A DIXON TROOP BOOK 3

KATHI S. BARTON

World Castle Publishing, LLC
Pensacola, Florida
Copyright © 2024 Kathi S. Barton
Hardback ISBN: 9798303546820
Paperback ISBN: 9798891263260
eBook ISBN: 9798891263277
First Edition World Castle Publishing, LLC, December 23, 2024
http://www.worldcastlepublishing.com
Licensing Notes
Cover: Cover Designs by Karen
Cover-designs-by-karen.com
Editor: Karen Fuller

Prologue

Londyn put the stack of books that she'd been using back. The law firm that she worked for didn't have the most up-to-date versions of them, so she mostly used her computer to find case material. After getting all the books put away, she was headed to her cubie hole to gather her things up and head home.

"Miss Rice?" She smiled at Donnie when he approached her. He was, she thought, one of the nicest people working at the firm. He worked in the mailroom and delivered the mail to the offices during the day. "I have some envelopes for you. I did find some about four months ago with your name on them, but I didn't hear back from you. Did you get them?"

"No. I don't know why I'd be receiving mail here. Do you know who you gave them to when you found them?" He told her that it had been Mr. Daily. "He's my direct report. Maybe he forgot."

"No, miss, he didn't. When I was going through the mail again about a week later, there were a couple more. He told me that he'd take care of them, but I've been watching him. The envelopes were put into his trash the next day." She didn't know what to think about that as she'd told Donny she'd never had mail sent here before. "I have them with me now. Not the old ones, but the new ones that came in over the last couple of months. I've been waiting to find you alone."

She didn't bother looking at the cameras that were all over the room. Not one of them worked. She knew that for a fact. As did most of the people working there. They were put in when she'd started here and never set up with the program that would make them run. Donny seemed to know that, too, and didn't try to hide what he was handing her from the white cameras.

"I don't know what these would be. Do you?" Donny told her that they had a law firm that wasn't this one on them, and a lot of them had insurance names on them. "That's really strange. All right. Thank you for giving them to me, Donny. I don't know what it could be about, but I'll look into them on Monday. I just want to go home and take a nap, then sleep for several days."

They both laughed, and he walked her to the bus stop. There were security guards that were supposed to do that for anyone leaving the building late, but she'd never been able to get them to get off their butts and help her out. She did wonder at times if it was because whatever they were watching on the little television that they brought in nightly had anything to do with it.

She was on the bus when she pulled out the first of the eight envelopes with her name on them. Not opening, fearful of what it might be saying, she stuffed them back into her bag and waited to get home. Whatever they were about, it had been this long. A few more minutes wouldn't make that much difference.

She got off the bus right in front of her building. Londyn had lived here since she'd gotten into college and knew the place and the people residing here like she did her own hand. As she was pulling out her keys, waiting just long enough for the man coming out to go in, she made her way up to the fifth floor, taking the steps two at a time. Which she thought was quite a feat, with her wearing high heels.

Changing her clothing to some comfy jammies, she hung up her skirt and blouse on the curtain rod so that it wouldn't get wrinkled. She didn't have much in the way of clothing. Two skirts, five blouses as well as two different sweaters that she wore when she was supposed to be going to court. She snorted when she thought of that.

Londyn hadn't been in the courtroom once, where she was the actual lead attorney. She could have been taking her own cases and making them work for her. But she'd been told, not less than a dozen times since working at Davis and Davis, that it was a man's world out there, and having a little bitty thing like her taking cases wasn't going to cut it. Also, she was told that the men of the firm all had families to support, and she'd just be taking food out of their families' mouths if she were to go to court. Londyn only had four more weeks before she'd be free of the obligation she'd signed when she'd gotten out of college.

Even graduating first in her class didn't give her any goodwill with the firm. She had resigned to the fact that it would be after she got out of this place before she was able to do what she had wanted all her life. Be an attorney.

After making herself a nice cup of tea, she opened up the tin of cookies that she'd baked last weekend. Londyn didn't allow herself too many of the treats. They weren't in her budget, nor could she make any more until her next week off. She was looking forward to the next four months.

There had been a retreat or something like a convention out in California, and the big-named attorneys were all going out there for the entire four months. She didn't know how they ever justified it, leaving the firm in the hands of the few people who weren't invited — her being one of them, but it was their thing, and she was just happy that they'd be all gone when she served her last day there. Having to calm herself down so she didn't dance, Londyn pulled out the envelopes again.

Using a butter knife to open them neatly — she had a pet peeve about people just ripping open an envelope like a savage and put them in order of mail date. The first one she pulled out was a firm by the name of Winston Jacobson Underwriters. Something fell out of the envelope, but she was too busy reading the letter to bother with it right now.

"Ms. Rice, I hope this correspondence finds you well. I wish to extend my deepest condolences about the

loss of your loved one, your grandmother. The insurance check is in this envelope, and that would conclude our business with the estate. Please let us know if there is anything we can do for you in the future."

Bending over, she picked up the check and stared at it for several minutes before she realized that it really was for just under a million dollars. Lying it back on the table, picking up the next envelope, she was astonished to find that it was nearly for the same amount, but the letter was saying that she'd lost her father.

Londyn didn't have any family left. She'd not had anyone since she'd been seven, and her entire family was wiped out in a flash flood that took their home down a long slope. Her grandparents had lived with them, and the ones that hadn't were already gone by the time she came along. Opening the other envelopes, she wasn't surprised that all of them were telling her that they were sorry for some member of her family and that there was a check.

Adding up the amount in her head, she laughed, a nervous one, when she realized that she had just under ten million dollars in check before her. They had her name on them, too, even with the strange spelling of London. Leaving them on the table, she went into her living area and turned on the television. There had to be some kind of weird shit going on because there wasn't any way that she had that much money. Especially since her family had been gone for nearly twelve years. And she'd been in the system in all that time she had been alone.

When she realized she didn't have any idea what was on the television, she turned it off and sat there in the dark. It was nearly three in the morning when she was startled out of her thinking when her cell phone went off. With shaking hands, she answered the call from Mr. Davis, one of the partners in the firm.

"What are you doing taking my mail home with you?" She asked him what he meant. "My mail. Not yours, and it's at your home. I wouldn't have thought you would be a thief, Miss Rice. Please tell me that you didn't open it. It could be bad for you if—"

"You mean the mail that has my name on it? The letters addressed to me that are about family members that I don't have? That mail?" He snarled. It scared her so badly that she had to change her phone to her other hand. She was shaking so hard. "I demand that you tell me why you have checks made out to me that I knew nothing about."

"You bitch. Now you've done it. I should have taken care of that little fucker Donny when he realized that I was having the checks come to me with your name on them. Well, there's no hope for you. I'm going to have to cut my vacation short. Go out there and kill the two of you for putting your nose in my business." She asked him what he'd just said. "Oh, don't get all squishy now. You should have just done what you were told and stayed out of the business of the big boys like me. Damn it all to fuck and back. And to think that I was going to give you a fat bonus come this Christmas. You'd better be there when someone comes for you, Londyn, or so help me, I'm going to enjoy killing you more than I should."

When the phone went dead, she tossed it across the room. How did he know? Kept going through her mind. Not wasting any time with that right now, she grabbed up the checks and envelopes and stuffed them into her bag. Going to her room, she pulled panties and bras out of her drawers and nearly screamed when her cat,

Maxi, leaped up on the dresser. Talking to the cat somewhat calmed her down. It also made her think beyond Mr. Davies telling her that he was going to kill her like he was quoting the weatherman about tomorrow's forecast.

"He's going to kill me. What will happen to you if he…well, he'll try and get you too. I don't know why, but he's just mean enough to…should I pack any food? No time for that. I have to get out of here." Picking up her cat, the only true friend that she had, ten minutes after the call, she was in the stairwell walking as calmly as she could with her favorite person, her cat.

Making sure that she had remembered to pick up her cash, very little of it compared to what she had in her backpack with her name on them. Londyn also remembered at the last minute to not bring the cell phone with her. As surely as the shows that she got caught up with in the evening, murder shows, there was going to be something in that cell phone that would give her away. She wondered briefly if they had tampered with any of the things that she now had on her.

Londyn was at street level when a long black car slid to a stop in front of the building. There were four men who got out, and then the car drove down the street, turned around, and headed back to the front door. No one tried to stop her, thankfully, and she just continued walking until she was out of sight of the building. Even from where she was hidden in one of the alleyways, she could hear the popping of guns. Or perhaps she thought that's what she was supposed to hear, so it was playing in her head. Her mind wasn't on right now. She was just too nervous to think beyond getting out of here in one piece.

She was just getting to the edge of town, Maxi following her now instead of being carried. He was fine to be hauled around when he wanted it. But not when she was in a hurry, it seemed. Christ, why didn't she just leave him behind?

"Because I love you, you big furball." He kept rubbing his head around her legs, nearly tripping her up when she heard a car coming. Slipping into the woods, thankfully, Maxi decided to come with her. She stood there against the trees as the big black car made its way out of town. While she didn't know where Donny lived, she wished that she had some way to warn him that he could be hurt. She only hoped that he was able to get away as she'd done. So far.

When the car paused, slamming on its brakes really, she stood as still as she could, holding onto the tree with one hand and the cat with the other. She even managed to hold her breath for nearly too long when she let it out as quietly and as silently as she could.

Maxi seemed to sense there was danger, so he curled himself up and around her neck, nearly making it impossible for her to breathe, much less see the car. When he backed up, flashing a huge light over the woods that she was hiding in, Londyn closed her eyes.

Like her not being able to see them was somehow going to translate into them not seeing her. Opening her eyes, she closed them tightly again when the light flashed over her tree. Not moving, so desperately wanting to take off running, Londyn stood her ground and waited. Finally, in what seemed like forever, the car took off again.

She didn't move out of the trees. Thinking that she was at least marginally safe since they'd not found her. Turning her back to the road, she made her way down the hill, careful not to fall and break something until she came to a clearing.

All kinds of things popped into her head then. Did they have drones looking for her? Was there a snipper just lying in wait for her? She was going to have to keep from watching those stupid shows, or she was going to be a basket case all the time. But instead of going through the clearing to God knew what else, Londyn sat down on the very edge of what she thought was summer wheat and leaned against the tree behind her.

"I'm in a pickle, Maxi. I don't know anyone to call who would want to come out in the middle of the night and rescue me. Because I don't know if you're aware of this or not, but we are in a pickle." Opening her pack up, she dug into it to see if there was anything that she could munch on. Finding a beef stick and a bottle of water made her a little leery. "I've never bought a beef stick in my life. But I must have, right? Want some?"

She kept talking to her cat, though she was careful not to talk too loudly. There were cars going back and forth on the road she'd been on, and she didn't want to alert anyone of her hiding place. Thinking how the beef stick smelled, she did think about if it would give away her cover, then hurriedly finished it off, giving a large portion to her companion.

The sun was coming up when she realized how exhausted she was. There were probably only a few miles between her and the town she'd been living and working in, so she was going to have to stay on her toes. Just as she was thinking that she had to pee, Londyn closed her eyes to let her mind settle a bit before she got up and moved on.

Chapter 1

Waylon didn't care all that much for being sued. Well, he was counter-suing, so it didn't really make that much difference to what the outcome was but he was assured by his attorney, his dad, that he was going to win hands down. He wasn't quite as sure as he was, but that was all right. So long as it was finished, he was glad too of that.

Douglass Brown was suing him because he couldn't get a house built without using him as a source for the wood and screws. Not to mention all the things in-between. Since he'd not waited on him hand and foot the day he'd come in for a five-cent washer, he decided that he was going to tell each builder that he got to talk to that they could build his home without using Waylon's hardware store.

"Mr. Dixon, I've read over the statement that you gave to your attorney and I think that there must be a typo in this. It says here that Mr. Brown was upset with you because you didn't go back and find the washer that he needed and bring it up to the counter in the first place. Is this correct?" He told his honor that it was true and also told him that Mr. Brown failed to get his house built because he wouldn't allow any of the builders to use him as a source. "I see. And is this a new thing? Having the store employees waiting on their customers instead of having them go back and find the item that they want?"

"No, sir. Not that I'm aware of. I did tell him were the washers were and even went so far as to tell him what size he'd need to replace the one that he had on him. But he was upset that I didn't go and get it for him. I was busy putting away merchandise and didn't figure that it would really be all that big of a deal." The judge told him that he didn't think it would have either. "So he's been unable to hire a construction crew to build his home because he tells them that they aren't to use me. I don't care one way or the other if he uses me or not, but the companies around — I give them a good deal on buying the entire needs of a house at one place, and I even only order things that will be used later down the line until they need them.

It's a win-win for everyone that places the orders, and I make out well, too."

"So let me get this straight, Mr. Brown. You've been blackballing Mr. Dixon here because he didn't do what you wanted when you showed up at his hardware store." Mr. Brown said it was more than that. "Then how about you explain to me what the difference is. Because as far as I can see, you're going to not get your house built because of a penny's worth of rubber."

"He wasn't all that busy that he couldn't go back on the shelf and get it for me. I told him that a lot was riding on him doing what I wanted." The judge asked him what the man had been doing. "I haven't any idea. He had this little dusting feather thing in his hand and was using it like it was going to be giving him some kind of magic. But it's the principle of the matter. I was going to be spending a great deal of money in his place, and he didn't seem to care about my money."

"I doubt very much that for all your blustering that day that it didn't matter to Mr. Dixon. Now, what is it you're suing him for, in your own words." Brown started out by complaining about how he had to park in the rain because he didn't offer any kind of pick-up and delivery service in the first place. Then he went on to say that since he was the customer who was in need of an item, Dixon should have been more accommodating. "Have you ever been in a hardware store, Mr. Brown? I mean one as large as Mr. Dixon's. and if you have, did they go and get what you wanted and bring it to you?"

"That's not the point. You see, I'm a paying customer that was going to spend a great deal of money in his place that he was willing to piss off because he wouldn't do what I wanted. The customer is always right." He was told that it was exactly the point, that he was thinking he deserved service that wasn't offered in any hardware store in the world. "And why not? Let me ask you. When you go into a store, do you want the best kind of service? Having someone cater to your needs? I do, and that's why I'm suing him. Because he didn't want to do what I wanted when I wanted it done."

"You're wasting my time here." He banged the gavel down on his dais and said that the case was dismissed. "Mr. Dixon, are you willing to let this go on your end if he tells you just what an idiot he's been. Not in those words, but close enough."

"He has been badmouthing me to several local construction companies to the point that they wouldn't build his home even if he were to use my hardware store. So I guess that's all right. Unless he tries this again." The judge looked at Brown and asked him if he was willing to let this go as he wasn't in the right.

"He bad-mouthed about me too. Telling the other construction companies not to work for me in getting my house built. I can't get my house built in town because once I put it out there that I didn't want this panty waste of breath to be any part of my home, they sided with him." The judge told him to move on. He wasn't going to be getting anything from him. "Well, that's not going to work for me. I want my house built."

"Then find yourself someone that will build it." Rolling his eyes, the judge looked at him. "I'm finding for the defendant, Mr. Dixon in this case and charging court cost as well as a five thousand dollar fine to Mr. Brown. See the cashier on the way out, gentlemen. Next case."

Waylon left with his dad who was disappointed in not being able to say a single word about the case. He decided to pay for his dad some lunch in compensation. He asked if he thought that he'd pay up.

"No. I mean, he'll have to pay at least the court costs, right? Then after that, there will be no money coming to me. I don't care, so long as he leaves me and mine alone from now on." They were just getting their lunch when his younger brother Cullen walked in with Logan, the supposed little boy that he'd picked up overseas when he'd been out of the country.

Logan was a magical creature that helped the family with things. Mostly, it was his brother Jayden and his new wife Hazel. They were the people to call when they had children who needed a good home for a temporary situation or even long term. The two of them had already taken in one child, an infant by the name of Allen. The entire family was in love with the little man and was spoiling him already.

"You look different today." Logan told them that he was fading into an older person, to be about thirty-five, so that he wouldn't have to hold onto the shape of a fourteen-year-old boy when he was considerably older than even Minx, who created him. It was not so much difficult but taxing for

him. "I think that will take some time to get used
to if you were to do it all at one time. You're very
smart for doing things this way."

"Thank you. We've come to ask you for a
favor. You don't have to do it, but there is a young
woman, I believe that you might have met her,
who is in need of a place to stay while she figures
out how to get someone off her tail." He asked
if he meant Londyn. "We do, as a matter of fact.
She's a brilliant attorney and is being hounded by
her former boss for the checks that were supposed
to come to her when her family was killed. It's a
goodly sum of money, too."

"I didn't meet her that day, but I did see her.
Dallas told me that she was on the run, but she's
also very skittish, too." Logan smiled. "You're not
telling me something, and I don't care to be—She's
my mate, isn't she?"

"She is. Telling you this now will be much
better for the two of you in the long run. I'm afraid
that if her boss, one of the Davis's of the Davis and
Davis law firm, finds her, he'll not just take her
money from her but kill her in a way that would
make it impossible to identify her in any way. I
believe that he's had practice. You do remember

hearing about young Donnie Lawson, didn't you? Well, he suffered greatly for his part in making sure that Londyn got the checks."

"Grandda said that he could smell that they were there at the house. Shot his mom while she was in bed, then tortured Donnie in a way that— like you said, it was hard to identify him. Why do they want the money from her? I mean, she's intitled to it, correct? There is no subterfuge on her part, right?"

"Every five years since the family was killed, the firm sends out another set of checks. She is the name on the checks, and they send them out with the banks, knowing that the pervious checks can't be cashed if the most recent one is being used. Or something like that. I'm not sure on all the details." It was Cullen who continued to speak. "They've been holding onto the checks at the firm until such time as she's killed. I think they were just waiting on her to be murdered by their hand, I'm assuming, so that they could go in and take the money as her attorney."

"They'd no doubt claim that they were the ones to be in charge of her estate and the ones that would pay out all the money. Sick bastards."

Logan agreed with him. "So? What do I do with my wealthy mate that anyone else couldn't have been able to do?"

"You need to claim her so that she's immortal. The sooner, the better." He told Cullen that he didn't care for being blackmailed. "I know you don't, but you can get to know her better after things hit the fan for her in the next few hours."

"You're serious. I need to claim her now, without even meeting her, so that she doesn't die and we can hang out together. That's a shitty thing to do to anyone. Much less your brother. What if you're wrong about her?" Logan said that he wasn't. "I don't like this. I'll do it because I don't want anyone to die for no reason. I know that ten million is a lot of reasons for her to be alive but I still don't care for this."

All he had to do was to say the words that would claim the woman as his mate. As he said, he'd do it, but he wasn't going to be hanging out with her anytime too soon. He had other things going on that needed his attention more than she might.

Once the words were out of his mouth, him claiming one Londyn Grace Rice as his mate and one true love, he felt a connection to her like a rubber band being snapped on his wrist. Standing up when he felt her pain, he looked at his brother and dad and said that he had to go. Once he was out in the sunshine, he realized that he hadn't any idea where she was or what was happening to her. Heading to the diner, where he'd first seen her, he stopped when he saw the large black car sliding to a halt near where he was standing. The passenger got out, and Waylon felt his gorilla snarling at the other man.

"You there. We're looking for that girl we asked you about. Have you seen her around lately?" He asked the man, a burly of a guy, why he'd think that he'd seen her since he asked him the day before yesterday. "We're not getting shit out of anyone around this town, yet we know this is where she is staying. You'd think that someone would help us somewhat. I'm her dad, and I've been looking for her."

"Father, huh? She must look like her mother if she's your daughter." He asked him what he knew about her looks. "You said she had purple eyes. You don't, so I'm assuming that her mother has them."

"Oh." He looked into the car he was still standing beside and spoke to the driver. He wasn't talking all that loud, but it was just enough for him to hear. He wanted to know if they should question him more someplace private. Unless he wanted a troop of gorillas on his ass, he'd better be rethinking that. He looked at him again, smiling a tight smile. "How about we get you a cup of coffee someplace and sit down and talk about this? I mean, you might have seen her and don't know it. What do you say about that?"

"I have to go to work." He said he was sure that his boss wouldn't mind if he was late. "I would. So no, I'm not going to go anyplace with the two of you."

When he walked by him, going to the diner again, the man reached out and grabbed him by the arm. All Waylon did was to look at his hand on him, then at the man. Smiling at him, Waylon let just enough of his gorilla go to make sure that man knew he was fucking with the wrong person.

"Remove your hand, or I'll tear your arm from the socket and beat you to death with it. I'm not kidding you right now." The man let him go, but not before showing him the gun that he had in his coat. "If you think you can pull that out before I can tear out your throat, then go right on ahead. I've got nothing but time on my side if it comes to having to kill you."

~*~

Londyn watched the exchange between the men just beyond where she was hiding. It occurred to her that this was the same man that had chased her down several days ago when she'd been hiding in the woods. Now that she was staying at the diner, the apartment just above the place, she could look all over the town and not be seen. It was nice, too, that she was nearly worry-free from the men trying to kill her.

There was no doubt in her mind that she'd be dead if they found her. Donnie had already been killed by them, and it didn't matter to them that his poor mother might not have known shit about what he'd done for her. She was also terrified that once they found her, Donnie's death would look easy compared to what they'd do to her.

The odd part was she'd not even known about the checks from the insurance company. Handing them over to Mr. Dixon, Dallas, his name was, didn't bother her so much as knowing that all this time, she could have been in a great deal better shape than she was now. Londyn had been living paycheck to paycheck since her parents had died and she'd been able to get out of college. She'd only had a few weeks left to work for the firm in order to fulfill her obligation for them paying half her college loans. She did wonder now if they'd ever planned to do that and it upset her that she'd worked there for a large pay cut just so they'd keep their end of the bargain. It was going to be difficult for her to trust many people after this was finished, hopefully without her being dead. That was what she was working for right now.

When the younger man moved away from the guy in the black SUV, she knew that some pretty harsh words were exchanged. Looking down at the towel that she'd wrapped her bleeding finger in, she was surprised to see that it looked as if it had stopped bleeding. Almost as soon as she unwrapped it to see if it was still bleeding a great deal, she had to close her eyes. The door to her apartment/hiding place opened she turned to find the man from the street there. Something Dixon.

"It's not there. The cut isn't there anymore." He nodded and moved toward her. Slowly, like he was gaging her temperament. "I nearly cut my finger off when I saw the big car...my finger is all healed up, and I'm not bleeding anymore."

She put out her hand when he asked her to. There was something so warm and comforting about him being so close. After he tossed the towel into the sink, he looked over her hand just to make sure. Snatching it back when he asked her if she was all right like he was asking her if she was sane, pissed her off. So she told him to leave.

"I was only asking to see if you were still hurting. I'm not sure how the magic works, but I was fearful that you might still have some lingering pain. The pain that I felt that brought me here." She asked him why he'd know she was hurt. "Yeah, about that. I knew because I claimed you to my dad. Usually, it's supposed to be to my older brother; he's the razorback in the troop, but my dad used to be the leader, and now—"

"You're babbling. What are you going on about?" He sat down after asking her permission. "Tell me straight up what it is you're talking about. How did you feel my pain? For that matter, how did you know that I'm living up here?" He didn't look like he was going to answer her so she kicked him in the foot.

"You're not nice. I knew you were up here because once I spoke to Janie, she told me that you were up here. Hiding out." So much for keeping her safe, she thought. "She wouldn't have told me but for the reason that I gave her."

"And just what reason that a perfectly strange man would be able to say to her that would allow you to come up here?" He told her that they were mates and that he'd claimed her. "What does that mean? I mean, I sort of understand, mates. I know a few shifters. But what does…you said that we're mates. Since when?"

"Since I don't know when. The fates made it so? I have no idea." She asked him what he knew about mates. "I mean, you know a few shifters. I'm a gorilla shift—"

"There isn't any such thing as gorilla shifters." He stretched out his neck, and she heard it pop several times as he stared at her. "I would think that someone would have said something about them before."

"So because no one told you that there are shifter gorillas, it can't be true?" He snorted. "Get over yourself. There are snake shifters, too. And in the event you didn't know, there are shifters for all kinds of animals around. Elite shifters also have the ability to shape-shift into things that have no heartbeat, too. I suppose you didn't know that either?"

"You're very snarky." He didn't bother answering her, and she was glad for that. "Tell me what this means, you claiming me."

"Just what you think it means. I've claimed you so that you didn't bleed out when you cut yourself. In looking at your hand just now, did you know that you also cut your wrist?" She said that her finger was ready to fall off, and that wouldn't have made her bleed out. "Oh, so now you're a doctor too."

"I don't like you one bit, just so you know that." He stood up, and she did as well. "Where are you going? Aren't you supposed to die without me next to you? That's all it's going to be too to by claiming me." Making his way to the door, he stopped suddenly, and she bumped him from behind. "What the—"

He turned to her quickly. His hand covered her mouth, and he held her tightly to his body. Nearly ready to unman him, she heard the voices, too. Several men were talking to Janie about her. Looking up at the man, she didn't have any idea what his name was when he told her to hush. As much as she hated to be treated like a child, she also didn't care to be told to hush like she was a baby.

"Logan is going to take you home." The man just appeared in the room. Sort of sprinkled in the room like he was some kind of faerie god mo — "Listen to me. He's going to take you to my house where they won't be able to find you. For the love of everything, will you stay put until I come for you?"

"Yes." As suddenly as the man came into her apartment, she was standing in a strange kitchen with boxes everywhere. "Where am I? And who are you?"

"I'm the elite shifter he was telling you about." She nodded, not sure if she was awake or something. "You'll be safe here so long as you don't leave the house for any reason. I'll return with your things in a few moments."

"I don't understand." He said that Waylon would tell her soon. "I'm assuming that's the guy who said that I've been claimed. Does he have any idea who I'm hiding from? Or why they're hunting for me? It was my money, and now someone is dead because of it."

She tried her best not to cry. She'd been doing that a lot lately since getting the checks from her estate is what she decided to call the money. Twice, she'd been tempted to hand the money over to the men, but she had a suspicion that they'd kill her anyway for making them have to find her. She was not sure why that kept coming into her mind. She was scared shitless about any bump in the night she heard too.

"You're going to be safe here. I swear to you." She asked about the man, Waylon. "He will be, as well as his family will be. They're all gorillas — please take my word for it that they're real. There are many things and many more creatures that exist that you will come to know and understand."

"I don't understand any of this now." He smiled at her and even though he looked to be in his mid to late twenties, she had a feeling that he was much older than he appeared. "Can you really change into a coffee table?"

"Shall I show you?" Shaking her head, she told him that she didn't want to know that bad.

"Suit yourself, Londyn. Now, if you wish, I can have one of the others come to sit with you. I'd like to go back and see to Waylon if you'd not mind. I don't think that he'll need my help, but I'm not entirely sure that the men with him will believe him when he tells them that he doesn't know you."

"I'll be fine by myself." She looked around the room. "Is he moving in or out? It could be about anything from what I'm seeing."

"This is his temporary home until he finds a home to share with you and your upcoming families." She said that she didn't have any family. "The one that you will create with him. I'm sorry, I must go. He does indeed need me there."

He disappeared, just like when he'd arrived, by sort of sprinkling out. There weren't words that she could think about that would be enough to explain to her what he was doing. Turning away from the now empty spot, she sat down on the living room chair and then jumped up. She needed to be doing something or her head just might explode.

There was a knock at the door that she ignored. Not even going to the peephole, she was terrified that once someone saw her eye in the little hole, they'd blow her brains out. She was going to have to stop watching those mystery things where someone is killed every episode, or she was going to drive herself insane.

By the time Waylon, using his keys, entered the house, she had tidied up his place and done the dishes that were in the sink. Not that it was all that messy, but she needed something to calm her nerves, and that was all there was for her to do.

"You're safe for now." She asked him what had happened. "What sort of person are you about someone giving you the full story? All at once or just a little at a time?"

"Did anyone else die because of me?" He told her that no one had died because of her. "Yeah? Tell that to Donnie and his mother."

"He knew that he was going to be in trouble when he handed them over to you. Perhaps not dead, nor his mother, but he was taking a chance, and that ended up with him being murdered. However, I will tell you that he'll be avenged before this is all over." She asked him how he was so sure. "Because to believe otherwise would be the same as giving up. You're not giving up, are you?"

"I don't know if this would be considered giving up but what do you think would happen if I were to just turn over the money to them. The checks, I mean?" he told her that they'd kill her anyway. "You sound so sure about that. It's not like I'd miss the money. I mean, I've been doing without for so long I don't know how I'd act if I had money for both groceries and my rent at the same time."

"Your apartment is gone. The entire building has been destroyed." She sat down hard on the chair again. "Also, your car. It was still in the parking lot when it was torched as well. No one got out."

"You need to work on your bedside manner." She stood up then and made her way to the kitchen to...well, she didn't know, but that's where she ended up standing. "All those people. They, for the most part, didn't know me, and now they've died because someone decided that me having the inheritance from my family all passing away was a reason to kill them off." She looked at Waylon. "They're really out to kill me, aren't they? For money."

"People have killed for less." She glared at

him. "You didn't answer my question about how to be told things, so I'm just not sugarcoating it. How do you want the rest of the information that I have for you?"

"There's a lot more?" He just stared at her. "Tell me. I have a feeling that getting it this way from you is better than hearing about it in the newspaper. What else is going on that I need to be aware of?"

"The people in the diner are going to be fine; however, you might want to know that they figured out that you were staying there. It's been burnt out as well." She felt her eyes fill with tears. "I've been told that they're going to have the money to rebuild but won't be doing that. The owner, Ms. Janie Scott, is going to retire and move to Florida when she's out of the hospital. Without Logan and myself there, it might have been a great deal more loss of life than just the two that had died. And since you asked, it was two of the men that had come looking for you that didn't get out." She told him good. "I thought you'd say that. They were killed by me as my gorilla. Logan helped to make it look like their bodies were simply in the wrong place at the wrong time. So no one will question why they were killed when the roof, your floor, fell atop them."

"Honestly and rudely, what do you think they would have done to me had they found me there?" He nodded and started to tell her. Putting up her hand, she asked him to stop. "You're much too blunt for me right now. Just knowing that they'd yank out my teeth one at a time is enough." She looked out the window again.

"For now, you're safe. The man, Mr. Davis, isn't going to let this go, so my family and I are going to talk to him about what's going on. And why his thugs were in the restaurant in the first place. The third man, the driver, has gotten away — mostly because we allowed him to so that he could go back and tell his boss that you're untouchable." She asked him if she was. "As of the moment that I claimed you, you became immortal. You'll be safe with me."

"But that didn't mean he can't get to me. Correct?" Waylon told her not to borrow trouble when everything else was free for her. "But they'll get to me. They'll try and kill me."

"Yes. But I'll protect you with my life from now on." She didn't know if she was all right with that either. She'd had enough people die because of her.

Chapter 2

Roman didn't care for the dead body in his office right now. It should have been three of them, but he wasn't worried about that right now. Rice, she was still out there and she had his money. As soon as he was able to put his hands around her scrawny little neck, he was going to squeeze the life out of her. Christ, it was a nightmare that was happening right now.

Glancing at the body that was just under the window in his office, he thought about tossing it out to the street below. But that would be dangerous as it was a nice sidewalk there, and people would notice that it had fallen from his window. He just hoped his dad or any of the other people in the office noticed it. He was going to do his best to ignore the body himself.

All Rice had to do was to work for him for the last year and a half or whatever her contract stipulated. After that, he'd have her declared dead, and that would be the end of it. He'd heard that someplace but didn't know how it worked. After seven years, you could have someone declared dead. No one seemed to be able to find her but him, and that was all right, too. Since he didn't want her popping up anytime after he had cashed out her checks, he actually was going to need to kill her. He'd been holding off in putting in his inground pool for months now so that he could easily dumb her body under the concrete, and that would be the end of his issues with his damned attorney.

She was a good one, too at least for as far as he would allow her to go. She did research better than anyone he'd ever met, and when one of his underlings went to court with her notes, they'd win hands down. If they didn't, he'd cut her pay again, and that, too, would make her have to stay under his thumb. Who would hire someone that couldn't even keep their pay up?

"Roman, have you found out what happened to little Miss Rice?" He nearly snarled at the man, his boss and father, who stood in the doorway, not coming in. "I've not seen hide nor hair of her since about a month ago. See what the holdup is in getting her to come in here. I know her place burnt down but there isn't any reason she doesn't come in and tell us what happened. Poor girl. She must be in a lot of pain or something is all I can figure. You do know that she's the only one that keeps you on the straight and narrow when you go to court with her research."

"She does not do my research, and nor is she the only one that...Dad, I can and do my own research when I have to go to court." To which he didn't add that was never going to happen again. "I understand that you like her but there isn't anything I can do if she's not answering her calls."

"Find her." When his dad stood there for several moments, staring at him, Roman wanted to wipe his nose. Even if he were to step one more foot into his office, his dad would see the coke that was all over his desk and the hundred dollar bill — only the best for him — rolled up to help pave the way for him to get stoned. "You have got a bit of powder on your nose, Roman. I've warned you before about doing that in the office where anyone can see you. Go home. Or better yet, go and find that girl."

He didn't need to be told twice to go home. As he was gathering up his empty briefcase along with his coat from last night, he was out the door and into the streets in less time than he took to try and figure out where he was when he woke up in his office this morning, naked and blurry-eyed.

By the time he remembered that he didn't have a car at the office, he was sweaty and pissed. It didn't take him long to be either nowadays, but at least he looked good while doing it. Roman knew that he'd lost a great deal of weight. He'd been a fat slob for most of his life and had only graduated from law school because his dad had a great deal of money. He no more knew the law than what his own phone number was.

"Mr. Davis, there are several messages for you. Also, we need to speak to you about your rooms." Holding out the little papers that were as pink as his eyes had been earlier, he took them from the butler and made his way to his rooms. He knew that still living at home at his age was pathetic, but it was free; he knew the address, and there was someone to clean up after him. As well as wash up his clothing. "Mr. Davis, before you go up, there is the little matter of Ms. Ambrosa Pennington."

"What about her?" He nodded in the

direction of the library and turned to walk away. He wanted to tell him to tell her he was still out, but she was standing there staring at him like he was some kind of insect under her microscope. Or was it a stethoscope? Like he knew what she did when out and about all day. "Hello, Amby. How's life treating y—"

The punch to his face took him off guard and had him lashing out at her almost as soon as she drew back to hit him again. But slapping her back, a huge mistake on his part, had her pulling out her gun and putting it to his forehead. He'd forgotten that, too. She wasn't one to mess around with.

"Now, Amby, we've talked about this before. No guns in the—what was that for?" She told him to stop talking to her as if she were a simpleton after popping him in the head with the barrel of the handgun she had. "I don't believe that I was. Put the gun away, and let's start over. How are the wedding plans coming along?"

"They're not." He wanted to leap for joy in not having to marry her, but he knew that if his father were to find out about this, he'd cut him off at his cock. "Have you seen today's paper, Roman? Or at least the front page? It's a very nice picture of you with your dick hanging out and your hands all over a hooker by the name of Loulou. It's funny that the headlines asked me the same question that you did. *How are the wedding plans going?* I'm finished with you." She turned on her heel but not before coming back and punching him in the face again. "I'm going to call your father right now and have this finished. I never wanted to marry you in the first place, but he promised me a large sum of money to do it. No way am I saddling myself with you."

His mind was centered on the *large sum of money* – just how much, he wondered – that she'd mentioned. Before he could get his mouth to work, his entire face hurting, not only was Amby out the door but he could hear her barking orders to the driver he presumed to take her to the Davis offices. His goose was cooked, as the old and odd saying went.

He'd forgotten about the body in his office before he could regret leaving the office so soon. What would the housekeeping people say when they ran across him? He was going to say that he didn't know anything about it as he'd been gone before noon. His dad would pitch a bitch about it, having to have the room cleaned, but he had more important things to worry about. That fucking cunt Rice and her checks.

It had taken him nearly four years to figure out that he could have gotten them sent to his firm. He'd concocted some story about how he had insurance, too, and there wasn't any point in them both doing the searches. When all the time she was working right there in the office for him. But the insurance companies, eight of them in total, decided that they'd be better served to find her on their own. That was when the checks started coming to his firm, eight of them over the next year. Well, his dad's firm for now.

Then that stupid shit Donnie had stuck his nose in where it didn't belong. Christ, the man had actually gone to Rice and handed over the checks that had come into the mail room when he'd explicitly told him to bring them to his office as he was looking over the accounts. Not that he'd get his hand dirty in killing him off, but it had cost him a pretty penny in getting the man dead so that he'd learn a lesson. Of course, he was dead, and that wasn't a good lesson for him to learn, but he was out of his hair for the time being.

Going up to his rooms, he was nearly ready to leave when he realized that his room wasn't made up and there was all kinds of shit laying around that he had wanted put away. Clothing, even some coke that he'd missed, was on his dresser. Making sure that he used up the smack amongst his underwear and socks, he went to his phone and called the kitchen. When no one answered, he was just ready to pull out his gun and shoot the lot of them. But that would piss off his father, and he had enough to deal with right now.

There had to be a way that he could go to the insurance company, and…well, he wasn't sure what he was going to do, but to tell them that he'd lost the checks wouldn't go over very well. They'd already put some stipulations on only Rice being able to cash them. They wanted her driver's license, birth certificate as well as her personally there to collect. He could get the other two but having her there? Well, that was the problem. That was when he came up with the plan to kill her off and then collect the insurance money after proving that she was indeed dead. That was going to be the highlight of his week, having her killed. He'd hated her since she was brought to the firm by his dad. And, of course his dad loved her the pieces. Roman just wanted to chop her up into pieces and be done with her.

Since he knew so very little about law and how to get around to collecting on the checks he'd had Rice actually look up on how to cheat her out of the money. Hell, he didn't even understand his Marandi rights when read to him at least once a week.

Nothing had gotten him into so much trouble that he decided to have himself driven everywhere so that he'd not first of all wreck and secondly to know where he parked his car. That had been a major problem for him, trying to remember where he'd parked and how much towing was going to cost him. Or his dad at least.

Then Rice had come to him with the fact that he couldn't legally collect checks when the person was still alive. After that, he'd been plotting her demise. Rice was one of the smartest women he knew, and yet she was the dumbest as well. Women were all stupid if anyone asked him.

Going to the kitchen, he found the big room empty. Even after looking everywhere he knew how to find his way around, he couldn't find a single person that worked there. After standing in the living room yelling for them, he couldn't get anyone to come. That was when he hit on the idea that he needed to get out of the house before his dad came home. It would be just like him to have not cleaned up his mess at work and had left the body there for him to take care of.

Not that he'd ever taken care of a body before. It was the first time he'd ever killed anyone personally. It made him sort of squeamish to see all that blood that came from the wound he'd inflicted and even more sick to his stomach when the body continued to twitch after he'd shot him. But it was all the man's fault. He'd made him kill him by losing sight of Rice and not bringing her heart to him after he killed her. So now he'd have to do it all on his own.

Roman had been of the opinion that if he didn't acknowledge something that happened, then it couldn't be true. Same with laws. If he didn't understand them, then they didn't exist. It had gotten him, with a good deal of his father's money, out of more situations than he could remember. All he'd wanted to do was to have some fun with people. His dad could never understand that, even after all these years.

After going to the garage, where there were usually at least five people hanging around doing whatever they got paid to do, it too was devoid of people. He was pissed off that he was going to have to drive himself to find his dealer. Since he'd stopped driving, he didn't know where to find him either. Christ, he hated all people today.

Just as he was pulling out of the driveway and was about twenty feet or so from it, several cruisers came up behind him only to turn into the driveway where he'd just come from. Whatever made the staff leave—he hoped they had a good reason or they sure were going to be in trouble when the police showed up.

It took him nearly three hours to find the house where he'd get his nose candy at—he secretly loved using all those terms he heard on the television and used them whenever he could. However, when he got there, it looked like the place had been raided. There was no one around there either. Also, it looked as if a fire had been set in the place across the street. Even the cars that were usually in the drive were burnt up. Knocking on the door a second time, it was finally answered by some construction guys or something. They asked him what he wanted.

"I have business to attend to here." He told him that they'd all been arrested and that he was there to get anything of value from the home before it, too, was torn down. "When? Damn it, why don't people notify me when this shit is going to happen. Did that old lady across the street have anything to do with it? I swear she was forever calling the cops on us...them."

"I can't help you, mister. The police come by here several times a day now, so you'd best be getting away from here unless you want to be arrested as well." The door was closed in his face, and that pissed him off as well.

Parking his car had been easy, but he'd left it running. A quick in and out, and he'd be on his way again. Now it wasn't starting, and he didn't remember to bring his phone with him. Walking back to the house, he knocked several times again to find out if he could borrow their phone to call his dad. He hoped that they had the number because he didn't have a clue about that either.

~*~

Londyn was nearly finished reading the

newspaper — just one more section when Waylon joined her in the living room. It had been a long time since she'd had the time to read an entire newspaper by herself. It wasn't much of a place that Waylon had but it was nice and cool as well as clean.

"There are some people looking for you. I haven't heard of the law firm but I'm assuming that it's the one that you used to work at." Waylon told her the name and asked her if that was it. After telling him it was, she handed him the newspaper but for the section on court dates. "There is a man named Dale Davis who has put an ad in the paper about finding you."

"I've not gotten that far yet. Have you spoken to him? Or know what he wants?" He said that he'd not, knowing that she was hiding from the younger Davis so he'd not kill her. "I liked his father. Mr. Davis is the one who hired me when I got out of college. Do you think that he's working with his son?"

"I have no idea. However, the note for you is in the section for cheap ads." He opened the paper for her, and she found it immediately. He'd even put her name in it, just to be sure, she thought that she'd get it. "It says to contact him through his personal number. I'm assuming that you have it since he mentioned that you're to call him."

"I did have it. When my place was burned up, my cell phone was in it. I was afraid to carry it around because I didn't know if Roman could track me or not." he told her that was good thinking. "Now that I think on it, I believe that he might not know how to do that. He seems pretty unfamiliar with not just cell phones but computers as well. The one that was on his desk had an icon on it to get into his games. That, I believe, is the only thing he used it for."

"He has a law degree, though. I would have thought he was smarter than that." She told him that he'd be wrong. "How can a man get through life without at least having a good working computer."

"I had one of the interns tell me that they had to set up his cell phone for him so that he'd only have to press a single number to call someone. While he wasn't even sure that he could make a call, he knew that one of the numbers was for a man by the name of Diesel. He was one of the drug dealers that would contact him occasionally while at work." Waylon wondered aloud again at how he'd gotten a law degree. "More than likely, his dad throwing money at the school. Or worse yet, Roman blackmailed his way to the top. And by that, I mean he was at the top of his class. I guess he figured that if he was going to get an education, he might as well have the best there was."

"If you don't mind, I'm going to make a couple of calls on your behalf. So is Amy, but I'll use her as a last resort. My dad is good friends with a great many people, too, so that might get you in closer than anything I can do." She asked him if it would get him into trouble. "Not really. Dad knows that he can turn me down, and if he does, I'll move on to something else. Also, will you go out with me to look at houses? I've had one in my mind, but it was sold recently, and I've figured out that I really didn't want it, or I would have tried harder. What kind of places do you like?"

"I wouldn't know. I've never in all my life lived in a house. I've been in them before, I mean, I'd go to other people's homes when I was a child but I've only ever lived in apartments since I can remember. Why do you need my input?" He told her. "I see. I guess I never thought of us getting that far in where we'll be living together. I thought that living here with you was just temporary."

"It is in a way. But I've been looking at houses for a while now. I can't stand to share things with my neighbor. Like noises that are coming through the walls. Driveways. That's another thing that I hate when someone takes up all the room in the drive when we're supposed to be sharing." She could see him getting upset when someone took more than their share of something. But she wasn't entirely sure whether it was a joke or not. She didn't know him at all, honestly. He'd done it to his brothers when there was only a single slice of cake left to eat and they were going to share. "I have three today to look at. Come with me, and I'll buy you dinner. I'm sick of fast food."

The two of them ended up getting coffee at the nearby market. She'd never been to it and was surprised at all the items that they had to offer. Not just coffee and tea, but there were scones as well as fresh fruit and veggie takeaways as well. She settled on a veggie cup with dressing to keep her from getting hangry if they were late getting dinner.

The first house on his list was a no. Even

pulling into the lumpy drive made her nearly empty belly feel off. The house itself was all right, she supposed, but there was more than likely a great deal of things to have done to it before it was livable. If ever. It was sort of a classic run-down place. No cars on the lawn, but there was a broken-down couch and a recliner on the front porch.

The second house wasn't much better. She wondered if the realtor had any idea who Waylon was. A wealthy man she knew she would have had to have made sure that he wanted to see houses that were at least the size of his parents and brothers.

"This is just laziness." She asked him what he'd meant. "Why we're looking at these houses. I told her that I wanted a fixer-up if it came to that, but I didn't mean that I'd have to tear down the building to start anew. That house, the second one, was in worse shape than the barn they found in the back of the property that Dallas bought. And it's hundreds of years old."

They were both laughing when they got to the third house. This time, they didn't bother getting out of the car. It had been burnt out sometime over the past few weeks, and the tape was still blowing in the wind from when the fire department closed it off.

They were headed out of town, thinking that they were going to have to find themselves another realtor, when she spotted a for sale by owner sign. Convincing him to have a look, it didn't take them very long to fall in love with the front yard and the wrap-around porch. Pulling up on the driveway there were two other cars there too.

"Are you here about the house?" Waylon told the older man that they were. "Just put it on the market about an hour ago and have already seen more people coming here than we have in all the years we lived here. Go on in, have yourself a look around, and tell me what you think."

Waylon took her hand into his as they went into the front of the house. The porch alone would have sold her on it, but upon opening the doors to the large manor of a house, she wanted to kick all the people out and tell them that she was buying it. There was a couple that was talking to what she assumed was the wife of the man in the yard.

As they walked around the large house, she overheard others talking about it. They were saying that the price was a little too high, but it was a wonderful find. Others, like her and Waylon, weren't saying anything to each other. At least not where people could hear them. They had their own conversations about it through their link.

The tiled front foray was perfect for the entrance to the house. The front two rooms, one of them what she would think would have been called a sitting room had old furniture in it that seemed to be something from the period of when the house was built. Even the library, brimming with books, caught their attention, as well as the floor-to-ceiling stained glass windows on both sides of the fireplace. It alone screamed at having a Christmas tree lit up beside it. As they toured the dining room, a spectacle of period pieces too, she could see them hosting dinners here with his family and not ever running out of room. She even loved the dish sets, about twenty-five settings that were in the four corner cabinets.

The woman came to speak to them, but she looked like her smile was tight. As if someone had said something to her and she was trying her best to be polite. Smiling back at her, the woman asked them if they had any questions.

"How much is the asking price of the house?" She told her and then went on to explain that the furniture that was out now came with the house. "I'm sorry, are you moving into someplace smaller? That's the only reason that I can see for you to leave such a grand house."

"Bless your heart, darling. It had been a hard decision to make but one that we should have made a decade ago. It's just too much for us, even though we have staff that comes in to help. There are five bedrooms on the upper levels as well as a large grand ballroom on the top. My goodness, it has seen some wild things going on up there." She took them on a tour around the bedrooms, waving them on so that she could take them to the upper levels. "My husband designed this house. It has so many features in it that I hate to leave, but it's necessary now that we're in our nineties, the two of us."

Margie showed them the whole house vacuum system. The dumbwaiters worked and came up to the upper levels easily. The hardwood floors on the third floor were enough to have her again kick everyone out and tell them that the place was taken.

"The kitchen is all modern. About a year ago, we decided that if we were going to sell it, we should at least make it look good. All the floors have had their carpets pulled up and replaced with temporary rugs. There is a washer and dryer on each floor, including the ballroom. You just never know when you're going to have to clean up some tablecloths after a party. Oh my, the things that we did in this house. Oh, you must see the porch around the house. In the back, there is a pool, of course. Inground because that was what we wanted. People were saying that no one would want to buy a house if it had a large pool in the back. Well, be damned with them all. We wanted to be able to play with the grandkids back there, so we put it in.

She showed them laundry shoots that were in each of the bedrooms that had been put in when the house was built. The wine cellar, as well as the craft room that she had down in the basement. Even the backyard was something to be impressed with. What with the orchard of apples and peaches there as well as grapes.

"We wanted this to be our forever home, and we nearly made it. But I want to have everything on one floor so that I don't have to worry about the stairs any longer." Waylon told her that he could understand that. "You're such a wonderful couple. I do hope you'll get it. Some people just don't appreciate the finer things in life." It was when her husband, Charlie, came into the house that she realized how much in love the couple was.

"We don't have to sell it right away. Some people, well, as I overheard my wife saying just don't understand that some people like the things are around here. One couple wanted me to slash, their words to slash the price of the house, or they were going to come in and burn all the furniture here so that it wasn't cluttering the place up with old stuff. Old stuff, indeed. Well, I hope they don't get it, is all I can say about that."

Londyn was sure that Waylon felt about the house the same way that she did. He was asking questions about acres as well as any other things that would pop into his head, seemingly without thought of the order of things. They were sitting on the back porch. It was very lovely with the pool right in front of them when Waylon made an offer on the house. To say that the Dutch's were surprised would have been an understatement. But they accepted even with the other offers that had been put in by some of the other people.

"I have to tell you, I didn't expect it to sell. I truly didn't. I thought that we'd be found in our jammies one night when no one answered the front door or something." Waylon said it was just what they were looking for in a new home for them. Then Charlie put out his hand before continuing. "I know you. I don't know if you remember me or not but I remember when you were just a little tyke under your granddas feet all the time. All you boys, you were such good boys and better men I hear now that you're all grown up. We used to go to some pretty grand parties at your parent's home, too, back in the day. Or I guess it would be your grandparent's day. My goodness, when I think of them, it makes me realize that I'm just getting older by the day."

The four of them had such a good time that Waylon invited the elderly couple out to dinner with them. She was starving by the time he convinced them to go, and they were going to meet the banker at the restaurant in order to sign off on the loan they were taking out.

Londyn couldn't have been happier. Now, if she could get that bastard Roman off her back, she'd feel a good deal better about life all the way around.

Chapter 3

The move didn't take them long, only about a week. The house was furnished and even the little bits and pieces that he had didn't take but a single truck to take it to their new home. They'd not realized when looking around the house that the Dutch's had moved out already and were just wanting to get it off their books, so to speak. After the paperwork had been signed, they were handed the keys as new owners of the Dutch Estate. Soon to be the Dixon Estate.

"When I can cash my checks, I'll pay for half the house?" He told Londyn that he had it. "I'm sure you do, but I want to have my name on the deed as well so that if anything ever happens to us, someone will be able to have a house to live in."

"I sometimes forget that you're an attorney." She asked him what that meant, and he laughed. "Nothing untoward about you. I just understand that you'd want to have all your i's dotted and all your t's crossed. I like that about you. And I also know that you're right that both our names should be on the deed. I wouldn't have it any other way."

He could tell that she was still unsure about what he'd said, but he was all right with that. They were having a good time making the place their own, and he wouldn't want her to feel slighted in any way about this forever home.

They were only going to need a few things before they could claim they were moved in. There was furniture, of course, but no linens. They decided to get themselves new mattresses as well as everyday kitchen plates and silverware. It was easy enough for them to get staff on board as the troop that Dallas ran was mostly older people who would jump at the chance of having a job so close to home. There were other details to work out, none of them terrible, but they were well on their way to get themselves situated into their home quickly.

Their new cook had worked at one time for his parents. But when she'd had to take over the raising of her grandchildren, she'd had to stop work to take care of the kids full time. He was excited to have Belle back with him. She made the best cinnamon rolls he'd ever tasted.

They also hired a driver for Londyn. He wanted her to have protection wherever she went until Davis was captured. He'd found out from his dad that there was a warrant out for Roman's arrest and questioning about a body that had turned up in his office. Dad said it also looked to him like Dale, his father, was taking precautions to have his only son out of the house permanently. Just as he was going to suggest that they take a drive to the Davis and Davis law firm, a courier came to the house with a cell phone in an envelope, especially for Londyn. She opened the large padded envelope as soon as it started to ring. He had her put it on speakerphone so that he could hear as well.

"Londyn? Is this Londyn Rice?" Londyn told him that it was her and what did he need. "Yes, I'm so happy you took my phone so that I can call you. This is Dale Davis of Davis and Davis. I had a feeling that something had happened to you and was worried that Roman had caused you bodily harm. How are you?"

"I'm scared out of my wits if you want to know the truth. Your son is trying to kill me over insurance money that was supposed to have come to me years ago. Now, not only am I worried about if he'll catch me or not, but to wonder at the lengths that he'll go to get me by burning me out of my own home." Dale said that he'd not heard about that. "My place is gone and everything that I had in it. Also, my car. It wasn't much, but it was mine."

"I'm so sorry, my dear. So very sorry. I should have known that somehow he would be involved in your disappearance. Not that this has anything to do with you, but he had a dead man in his office this morning when I found him. He didn't say a word either. Just left for the day, and when I went in there to talk to him about finding you...you can imagine my surprise." She told him about the two bodies that had turned up in her apartment when it was burnt up. "I swear to you, honey. I knew that he was a bad person but I just didn't know how bad he was until all this. And he's been searching for you too. I heard from your father-in-law. He was going to do something for me about my son or to help me with him when he told me about him having your insurance checks waylaid from you. My goodness, I never expected...well, I suppose no one expects their child to be a monster. And that's just what he is. A monster."

"I'm terrified for my life. And from what I've heard, I should be afraid." He said that he'd do anything he could to help her. "Did you call the police when you found the dead man?"

"I did. It was in my head, I have to tell you that I wouldn't do it. Somehow making it justified in my mind about him. But how does one do that? Justify their child killing someone when there was no reason for it. I called them right away, and they're looking for him." She told him good. "I also have changed the locks on my home, stopped him from having a driver, and anything else that was on the list that Sherman gave me. He's upset with me as well. A good man that, Sherman Dixon. And now he's helping me turn the tables on Roman to get him arrested."

Mr. Davis told her that he was working with the insurance company to get her the rest of her money. That had been a surprise to find out there was more money coming her way. After struggling to be able to eat and pay the rent, now she had more money than she knew what to do with. Dale, as he asked to be called, asked her to hold on as he had a call coming in on his house phone. She did so without putting up any kind of fuss.

"You're going to be happy to hear that Roman has been arrested. He's currently in a jail cell in Columbus, where he was caught trying to steal a car. His excuse with that one being that he couldn't find his own so he took what he needed." There was a little hiccup of a sound, and she knew that he was crying. "I raised him to be better than this. I want you to know that. I wanted him to be a partner with me in my firm, but all he ever did was lash out at the others there and treat them as his own personal servants. I did indulge him a bit more than I should have when it came to his education too. Oh my, what have I done?"

She didn't interrupt him in his crying. She'd cry, too, if she had a child that was as bad as Roman. But there was very little that she could do about it now, so she thought that moving on was her next step. Then she asked what he was going to do about helping her with her insurance money.

"I'll get the checks in the morning delivered here. Once they're here and certified to be correct, the underwriters of them will hand them off to you. You'll have to be careful with them. They're certified checks, which, I'm sure you understand, can be cashed by anyone who has them. You should get those Dixon boys to take you to the bank to get the money distributed for you. They're gorillas, and that will make you safe and sound." She looked at him, and Waylon told her that she'd have nothing to worry about. "Good for him. Women like you don't come around all that often but I'm so happy that you have yourself a good man in Waylon. All his family are good people."

"I'm beginning to see that." After they had finished speaking, she handed the phone off to him. Waylon made the arrangements for Londyn and his family to go to the offices tomorrow. Just knowing that Roman was in jail, he knew that he'd sleep a good deal better than he had last night.

Every creak of wood, every snap of rain against the window, woke him up. Not only did he not sleep well because of Roman, he was pissed off at the man for making his mate so upset. After closing the phone, he went to find Londyn. He found her in the kitchen making herself a cup of hot tea.

"I don't care for it, to be honest, but there is something about making it that makes me feel less tense. Not that I'll simply dump it out, no, I'll drink it but I do feel better once I sit down to drink it. I believe there are cookies somewhere, too." He pulled down the large tin and handed it to her. "I'm not even going to ask you why you knew that this was up there. Did you, by chance, sweet talk Mrs. Dutch out of knowing where it was?"

"I put it there when I came down here this morning, and our cook, who I like, by the way, was baking. I put them in the stash so that even if my brothers came over to snitch a few, I had our own special stash right there." He took one of the iced treats and bit into it. "I'm hoping that you'll have dinner with me tonight. The cook told me that she'd need to have supplies brought to the house, so I'm assuming that there isn't enough to make even a sandwich."

"I don't know. How about we order something and have it delivered. I need to feel safe here at home. I know he's in jail, but just the thought of him being out there gives me the willies. How about a large meat pizza and some nice wine?" He thought that was a splendid idea and set about making it happen. "I believe I saw a couple of bottles of some wine in the basement. I'll go there and get it now."

While she was getting the wine, Waylon

decided to not just order pizza but was going to have some desserts delivered as well. Finding a place that would bring him some cheesecake, he ordered an entire cake and thought that it would be nice to just have some around to eat on when they wanted a treat. He knew that it would freeze nicely and he sort of liked the frozen confectionery too.

They ate, sitting on the floor in front of the fireplace, watching television. It was much too warm out to have a fire but it was nice to just sit and have some quiet time. Waylon was more than a little bit happy that she suggested ordering in. It was certainly more relaxing than having to drive someplace and back again.

Clean up was put off in favor of just sitting around. Leaning against the couch, he was just closing his eyes when he heard from Cullen. There was going to be another child brought to his brother, and he wanted to know if he wanted to join them at the hospital. No biggie, he said, as no one else was planning to go either.

"I think that we're in for the night." He just then remembered that his family was supposed to come over later to have a look at their new home.

"*I'm assuming that the plan to come here is off as well.*"

"*I forgot about that. Yes, I would assume so. But a new child in the family is good, right?*" Waylon remembered his other brother Jayden telling him that they were going to be taking in children all the time now and wondered if they'd get to keep this one. "*He's about ten, the little boy is. His parents were both killed in an automobile accident about a month ago. Todd is only just getting to the point where he can get around. His grandparents are making arrangements to come and get him in a week. As you can imagine, it's been hard on all of them.*"

Waylon let Londyn know about the new addition, if only for a week that they were going to get. Like him, she'd forgotten about them all coming over to see the house and got up to clean up their mess. It wasn't much of one, not really, but like him, she didn't care for clutter.

Getting up to get onto the couch, he realized that it wasn't as comfortable as he might have thought it would have been. Deciding that he was going to get them something else, something that went with the house, he wondered how the elderly couple was able to have a nice relaxing sit down when there were springs popping up everywhere.

Waylon thought that after all this time, they more than likely knew where the bumps and springs were.

~*~

Londyn was nervous about being in the office again. Dale told her that her things had been boxed up and that he'd make sure that they were sent to her new home. He seemed to be as excited about their purchase as they were. When the underwriter came to make sure that she was indeed Londyn Grace Rice Dixon, the checks were handed to her one at a time so that she knew who the insurer had been as well as the person who had taken out the policy. The checks that she had on her at the time were null and void because they'd been tampered with. Not by her, but they'd been in the possession of too many people for him to feel comfortable to have her have them.

"Now, these last checks are for the double indemnity on their deaths. The insurance company that was for the hotel that your family was staying at and the hotel itself have agreed to pay the amounts of the insurance on your family. They were found negligent on all accounts and have had to pay out for everyone that was lost that day." She asked how many others were hurt or killed that day. "Nearly everyone staying at the hotel. About three hundred people total."

"That's terrible." He asked her why she wasn't with them. "I was in the hospital with the pneumonia. I was to join them the day after they were all killed. I begged them not to go. But my mother explained to me that there would only be a couple of days that I'd miss them and I'd be fine in the hospital. I think about that on occasion."

"My goodness, child. As much as I'm sure you hate that you lost your family, it's good that you were spared of the mudslide. I'm to understand that the hotel was the only business that was completely taken out. Lots of homes, too." She said that she thinks of that daily. "I'm sure you do. I'm positive, too, that you take that on as a bad thing. No, you're lucky. Why think of all the things that you've accomplished since they've been gone."

"I do." She wanted to move on from the conversation and was glad when Waylon seemed to have understood that. Once he started talking to the man, Mr. Robbins, she was able to gather her thoughts up and slide her way into thinking like he did. That she was very lucky to have been sick.

Going to the bank, the people there were falling all over themselves trying to help her. Finally, getting into the office of the bank manager, she was able to not just get an account opened up but to put Waylon's name on them as well.

"I can't believe that I have this much money." Waylon told her that it was smart of her parents and family to have made sure that they were insured, too. Not to mention her not being there when it happened. "What would have happened to you had I died? Would you never have found a mate?"

"I don't know, to be honest with you. Someone else might have come along. But knowing you and being in love with you—because I am with all my heart, I can't imagine they'd make me as happy as you are right now." She wanted to kiss him. To show him how he made her feel, but before she could get up enough nerve to do it, he pulled her to him and kissed her.

It was a good kiss, and she was glad that he'd done it. But it hadn't been enough. Not nearly enough for the way she was beginning to feel about the big man. After finishing up with the bank, they went to Jayden's house to meet the newest member of the Dixon family.

At once, she didn't like him. Even when he put out his hand to shake hers, she wanted to find a place and wash up not just with soap but with any kind of disinfectant that she could find, too. Once they were introduced, Hazel asked if she wanted to see the baby. Following her out of the room to see the little boy, who was just a month old now, she was slightly confused about why she hadn't brought the baby down for Waylon to see, too.

"You don't like him." She just stared at her. "It's all right. I don't either. I'm sure there will be times when someone comes to our home, and we'll not like, but I feel like he's looking for a place to stab me in the back all the time."

"I didn't get that but I did take an instant dislike to him. I thought that it was just me." Hazel shook her hand and handed her little Allen. "Now, this little guy I like already."

She was playing with the little boy when Todd, the little boy staying with them, came into the room. He told Hazel that he was hungry. Telling him that he could wait another ten minutes for their lunch had him stomping his foot and telling her now.

"You won't speak to me that way, young man." He told her to shut up and get him something to eat. "Logan, come to me."

Logan, a man that she'd gotten to know over the last few days. She didn't take her eyes off Todd when she told him that the little boy was out of line. While she knew that Logan had magic, a great deal of it she'd been told, he simply disappeared with the younger child. Londyn looked at Hazel.

"Where did they go?" Hazel burst into tears and told her that she didn't care so long as he wasn't there. "Has he hurt you in some way, Hazel? Maybe he has taken his temper out on you? I'll take care of him if he has."

"No, nothing like that, yet." It was the yet that scared her the most. "Allen screams his head off whenever he's near him. Like he somehow knows something that we don't. Also, last night, I heard him talking to the baby over the intercom system. I didn't hear what he was saying but Jayden did and jumped out of the bed and went to bring Allen to us to sleep with. I've never been afraid of children before, but this kid...he really creeps me out."

"You're also thinking that he had something to do with his parent's death, aren't you?" She nodded, using one of the tissues off the changing table to blow her nose. "What has he said? I mean, when you called Logan, he didn't even ask questions about anything but took him away."

"I told him how I was feeling about the little boy. And while I can do it, I've not searched his mind. Not that I can't, but Jayden is much better. He's only been here for two days, and I want him to go away forever." She played with Allen to sort of distract herself from thinking about what was right there in front of her mind. "I have a feeling that the grandparents won't last all that long, and he'll be right back here. I'm actually terrified of that. What will he do if I tell him no again? It's only lunch, I know, but I also know that he'll not like anything that we have for him. None of the toys that we have are good enough because we didn't buy them just for him. I'm afraid of him, Londyn. And I'm a grown woman."

She told her what she felt when she shook his hand. "Also, when he came up here demanding lunch, I found myself wanting to smack that smirk right off his face when you told him no. it's like

he's keeping track of what you tell him no about."
She looked around the room. "I'd not leave the
baby alone for anything if he's around. That's a
terrible thing to say, but that's just what I feel."

"I do as well." Logan appeared in the room,
but he was alone. Hugging Hazel, he told her that
Todd was being watched over by Minx until such
time that his grandparents were here. "Will she be
all right? I'd hate for anything to happen to her
while he's with her."

"She has a great deal of magic and will keep
him in line." Logan looked at her. "You're all right,
aren't you? I mean, he didn't hurt you while here,
did he?"

"No, nothing like that." She was handed a
bottle for the baby and was content to rock and
feed him. But she did have one question. Not
looking at either of them, she finally had the nerve
to ask. "Did he kill his parents? Make them have a
car accident?"

"He did. He was upset about the fact that
they weren't going to be able to buy him all the
toys that come with the meals. They don't have
them all in at once, they tried to explain to him,
and when the opportunity came, Todd put his

hands over his father's eyes while he was driving, and the impact into a semi-trailer took both their lives. He was hurt badly himself, but he survived. I've made it so that there will be an inquiry about the accident, and they'll figure it out with a little help from me." She asked him if he'd done things like this before. "Yes."

For some reason, she was content with that answer. It was frightening, but that's all she wanted to know. Whatever the kid was about, someone needed to get a handle on him before he killed someone else. And for as sure of her new love for Waylon, she was sure that the boy had killed before.

After giving the baby his bottle, they went to the living room. The nursery was set up so lovely that she wanted to go home and decorate one of her own. Like that made sense. She didn't even have a baby, not to mention she'd not had sex with Waylon. And she realized that she really did want that to happen, too.

They ended up staying for dinner, too. She watched Jayden change Allen's diaper and thought it funny that he had to keep referring to the pictures on the box to do it correctly. During her teenage years, she'd done a lot of babysitting and was able to impart a few tricks to them that they could use. Jayden hugged her three times when she told him it wasn't necessary to take his sleeper all the way off to change him. The silly man.

Heading home, she realized that she was very excited for the family. Excited, too, that she'd be able to have family around her for the first time in over a decade. Since the night was so warm and they could, she and Waylon decided to take a swim in the pool. She didn't have a bathing suit but realized that she could change into anything that she wanted. Going down to the pool, she was nervous to see that Waylon was already in the large pool and swimming laps.

Seeing him this way, half naked with water streaming down his chest. It took her several seconds of not breathing before she was able to move toward the deck chairs that they had. When he saw her, he came to the edge of the pool and smiled at her. There was something so utterly amazing about seeing a half-naked man in a pool that made her mouth water.

"Are you all right?" She told him about how she discovered that she could wear and change into anything that she wanted. "I didn't think of trying that. I just realized that you don't have much in the way of clothing, do you? What with your apartment going up in flames."

"I have a few things that were at the dry cleaners when I went to pick them up. Not too much for everyday wear. But I was able to order me a few things while I was hiding from Roman. Everything that I ordered came to the diner and under her name. They were really good to me while I was hiding out there. For money I would help with the busing tables and doing the pots and pans."

"I never thought of you not having credit cards either. This with your money, it must make you feel pretty good?" She said that she felt wonderful and that she was happy too that she had all her money where it needed to be as well. "My mom is great at investing money. You should talk to her about making every dollar work for you. I know she's made me a bundle by listening to her advice."

"I'll do that." She was tempted, really tempted, to ask him to get out of the water so that she could have a full view of him. But instead, she made her way to the deep end of the pool, where the diving board was, and dove into the water. It was almost too warm, but it was heavenly on her poor body after all the things that she'd been stressing about since Donnie handed over her money that fateful evening.

When she had enough splashing around, she started to the stairs. It was then that Waylon came to her to mostly help, but when she slipped backwards, her body hitting the water hard, he was right there to rescue her. And he held her in his arms until she stopped trying to stand up again.

"Are you all right?" She nodded and had to swallow twice before she could form words. She told him she was just fine. "Good. I was thinking that if you'd not mind, I'd really like to make love to you. Not right this second. There are too many prying eyes around here, and I don't want to have our neighbors pissed off at us before we even get to meet them. But the thought of taking you upstairs to our room and having a great deal of sex with you appeals to me in a way that I'm hard just thinking about it."

"Okay." He laughed, then simply threw back his head and laughed loudly. Getting out of the entanglement of his arms, she stomped her way to the house. He'd learn not to make fun of her again.

Chapter 4

As soon as they were in the screened-in back porch he knew that she was upset. However, how upset she was, he couldn't judge. Walking toward her, taking off his clothing as he made his way to her, she inhaled sharply when he pulled his shirt off his body and let it lay where it dropped.

"I'm mad at you." He asked her if she was mad at him or just sexually frustrated. "How am I supposed to know? I've never had sex before. I mean, I've had sex, just not had a climax. I suck at being sexy, too, just so you know."

"You could be in a burlap sack that was smelly and old, and I'd think you were sexy as hell." She smiled at him, but he could tell that she was still upset. "Have I told you how much I love you? I do. With all my being. And I will love you forever, too."

"That's very sweet of you. But what if we're not compatible?" He started to laugh but caught himself in time. He didn't realize until that very moment that she was as insecure as he was confident in his love for her. "Are you laughing at me?"

"No. I'm amazed if you want to know the truth. I can't believe that anyone you had sex with wouldn't do everything in their power to make sure you had enjoyment more than them. I live for making you first in all things." She asked him if he was serious. "I am. Right now, my only pleasure would be to make you enjoy us making love to the fullest."

Waylon pulled her toward him and kissed her. Her mouth was wet and warm, her tongue tangled with his over and over until he felt as if he'd touched every part of her. He was doing exactly what he wanted. He needed to claim her. Reaching down, he spread his fingers along her back and pulled her closer, her breasts pressed against his bare chest. When her hands moved up his shoulder to his hair, he shifted her until she was riding his thigh. Cupping her ass, he pulled her up and down his leg until she moaned. He tore his mouth away and put his forehead onto her.

"I want you. I want to take you right here

and right now. I can't seem to get enough of you. Touching, tasting." He stepped back and dropped to his knees before her and pulled her to his mouth, bikini bottoms and all. "You smell delicious. I want...I need to eat you."

He yanked her bottoms down to her knees and buried his face into her soaking curls. When she curled her hands into his hair again, Waylon couldn't have stopped if someone put a gun to his head.

Sliding his fingers up and into her wet sheath, he fucked her as he suckled at her pussy. The warmth of it, the heat of her, was making her flood his mouth with all the cream that he wanted. And he found that he wanted it all. When she pulled at his hair, he looked up at her and growled low.

"Not here." He looked at her, confused. "Not out here where the neighbors can see what we're doing. Please? Let's go into the house. I don't even care if there is a bed involved, but I don't want to make love to you right here in the open where people can watch us."

Standing up, he picked her up in his arms. He nearly tossed her over his shoulder but realized that if he were to just turn his head to the right ever so slightly, her pussy was right there for him to taste again.

The living room deck door was hard for him to open. First of all, he knew that he wasn't seeing what he should be doing, and secondly, he knew that if he didn't get her someplace right away, he was going to not give two shits about who saw them. He and his gorilla wanted her so badly that he was weak in the knees just thinking about it.

Finding the couch, he put her down and bent her over it. The site that greeted him was her lush, plump ass. Bending over her, shutting the door — none too easily either — at the same time, he licked a path from her dimples to her pussy and back again. Her moans and begging were getting the better of him, and he didn't want to rush things too quickly for her.

Leaning over her, he wasn't surprised to feel her backing up to have him take her harder. Filling her pussy this way, filling her from behind, he noticed that he could see her breasts as they swayed while he took her. The beautiful orbs with her hard nipples swayed back and forth in time to his fucking her, and he was so lost in the movement that he nearly missed her first climax.

"Holy, Christ, I'm coming." She screamed out his name. Even as he fucked her faster, harder, he reached down between the two of them and cupped her breasts in his hands. Toying with her nipples, all he wanted to do was suckle them until he passed out with the pleasure of it all. And when she came a second time, he bit down on her shoulder, using it as a lifeline so that he'd not come apart too much. Waylon emptied himself deep inside of her even as she cried out that she was coming again.

When he woke up, he was lying on the floor. There was a throw over him, for which he was glad for while he looked around for Londyn. She wasn't anywhere near him but he knew she wasn't far. Sitting up, he had to lie back down twice before he could feel safe enough to move much more than he already had. Christ, he was sore and exhausted.

"I'll help you up, but you can't touch me." He grinned at Londyn, telling her that he had to touch her to get up. "My body is still buzzing. I mean, even going to the bathroom a few minutes ago was too much, and I swear to you, I came while I was peeing."

"That's not sexy, yet it is at the same time." She helped him up but she backed away from him quickly, nearly tripping over the footstool that was just behind her. "Careful there. I don't want anything to happen to you."

"If that was what a regular climax feels like, I can tell you for sure that I've never ever felt like that before. While I'm sure that it was special between the two of us, I don't believe that we can have sex like that again for a while, however. I'm sore, too." Using only his heels, he made his way to the bathroom, asking her if she needed him to help her up the stairs. "I just told you I'm sore. How on earth…that was very nice of you, but no. I'm going to go upstairs and run a hot bath. I can't believe that you're walking around at all. I love you, but no, please don't touch me right now."

When he finished up in the bathroom, he made his way to the upper levels. Now that he was moving around, he did feel better and by the time he was up the stairs, he didn't hurt at all. But he knew that a nice warm shower would take out the rest of his kinks, should they appear tomorrow, and waited until Londyn was finished with her bath by sitting on the commode and talking to her.

"Just so you're aware, I've never come like that before either." She was washing her legs by bringing them up out of the water to the point where he could see her thighs. "You're the most sexy creature that I've ever seen. And I love you."

"I love you so much, too." She frowned a little, and he nearly asked her what was wrong when she spoke again. "I'm an attorney. I know you're aware of that but I was thinking that I'd like to do some cases for your family. To help them out if they need it. I know your dad is one as well. Maybe we can work together. What do you think?"

"Let me ask you this first. Do you want to work, or do you think you have to work? You don't if you don't wish to. My mom does a great deal of charity groups and is on the board of a lot of the businesses around town. Like the library and the hospital. Also, she does a great many fundraisers throughout the year as well." Londyn said that she did notice that she was busy all the time. "I was thinking too that you could come in and work the hardware store with me but I'd be closed more than opened. Chasing you through the shelves would just be too much fun not to try. I don't know that my parents could work together either. Dad's not very neat when he works at his desk, and it drives my mom nuts. Her area, usually the dining room table, is neat as a pen, and she knows just where everything is."

"I would enjoy going to see where you work sometime but you're right, we'd never be able to sell anything if you and I are together for very long. Even though I'm still a bit sore, I can see us having fun like we did downstairs against the cash register." He laughed, telling her that was just the way he'd take her too. "I need to work. I can't be idle for long before I start down the path of being depressed. I've had depression all my life and low self-esteem. The only reason that I was able to do what I did was that I kept telling myself that it would end soon and I'd be on my own as an attorney. That's all changed now. I still want to be one but I want to work for a single family, yours. Will you get in the tub with me?"

"Yes." Once he was in the water behind her, he washed her arms and shoulders while thinking about how to answer her. "Dad would love to have you with him on things like that. He doesn't go all that often, but when he does, he usually wins. Also, it would be good too to have you around as you'd be able to read contracts. We usually have a couple of those we need to go over a week for one thing or another. I don't know that you know this but I also own General Hardware. It's a place that I worked at for a long time as a kid so when the time came up for it to be sold off, I bought it and didn't change a thing. It works well in keeping me busy, as you said. I've only just realized that you probably know very little about my family. Do you?"

"No. I mean, I've heard bits and pieces. I know that Dallas works at the zoo, and that's how he met Amy. She's a photographer." He told her that Dallas was part owner of the zoo and that he had a doctorate in animal husbandry. And that Amy takes pictures of zoo animals so they can be made into calendars to sell. "I didn't know that much at all."

"Jayden used to teach but is now the administrator for the district. He has his office right there in the building with the little kids. He'd been the teacher of the year for about five years in a row before that. He wants to be in the middle of — Also, I just thought of something. Amy's brother is the president." She asked him of what. "The United

States. When we were trying to find your boss, Jamie, that's his name was the one that got us into some of the buildings that Roman was in. He also has extra guards on him for us because you're not officially, but you are a part of Amy's family. We're all under surveillance with the Secret Service all the time."

She turned and looked at him. "Are you serious right now? I mean, the president of the United States helps out this family?" He pointed out that she was a part of the family as well. "Yeah, sure, by about a million times removed. She really is his sister?"

"I wouldn't kid you about something like that." She nodded and went back to playing with the bubbles in the tub with them. "Let me see. Booth teaches Spanish at the high school. He can teach a lot of languages but that's on the curriculum right now. Falkner, as you know, is still living at home, working on becoming a doctor. He's decided that he wants to be a pediatrician/OBYGN doctor when he gets out, and we're all proud of him."

"And Cullen? What's he doing? I know that he's home from some place but I don't know that I ever heard from where." He told her just as they were both getting out of the tub. She paused when he handed her a towel. "What do you mean he's just a serviceman? I'm pretty sure that if he's a Dixon, he's not telling you the entire thing. He must be something like special ops or a green beret. You guys are much too competitive for you to be just plain old anything."

"I didn't say he was a plain old serviceman. I just said that's what he is. And the only person that would know anything like that would be Dallas. He's the closest to him." She was mumbling something about Cullen running for president someday as she snatched the towel away from him and dried her body like she was angry with it as well. "Honey, you're going to rub your skin off if you keep that up."

"You drive me crazy." When she stomped her foot at him, he couldn't help but laugh. Storming out of the bathroom, he went to find her while drying off. He didn't know why she was so upset but he was willing to bet it was going to be his fault. He found her on the bed sobbing. He asked her what was wrong. "Nothing. Everything. I'm just...and I am just a plain person that you tried to save. You guys know presidents, are land

and business owners, and I'm barely cutting it by hanging around you. I have money but only because my...are you laughing at me?"

"You've had money since the moment I met you. As for being a business owner, you also own the hardware store. I put your name on the business and the deed. And as for your family money, honey, you could toss it all away for all I care. Having you to hold and to love is the best I've ever thought to have in a mate. You're loving and kind. Smart too. I'd put you against my dad any day of the week if you had to go toe to toe. As for Cullen running for president, believe it or not, Dallas is working on that very thing. Jamie is helping him fill in the gaps of what he needs to do so that when he steps down in a few years, he'll know that the torch has been passed to him, and he'll make sure that things go just the way that the two of them have planned out. Why, I'd bet that Jamie would run as his running mate if I had to guess."

"I love you." He kissed her on the nose and pulled her body to him. "I have to ask you one more thing then I'm going to sleep. What happened to Todd?"

"You mean the little boy that Hazel called Logan about?" She asked him if he knew any more Todds. I do, as a matter of fact, but you're right. I should have known who you were talking about by the way you keep changing the subjects—ouch. That flipping hurt."

"And I'll pinch you again if you don't tell me what I want to know." Her smile got him. He could live on that for the rest of his life without food if need be. "Well?"

"He's gone." She rolled her eyes and threatened him again. "What I mean is, he's been taken care of and put in a prison for the rest of his life. He did kill his parents, along with the neighbors, to the right of their home. Not only that, but Logan was able to find where he had plans to kill off Jayden and Hazel as well as the baby. Not that it would work, but he had a very sick mind. And a very spoiled way of looking at things. I'm glad that you and Hazel talked that day, or there is no telling what might have happened to them."

"I'm glad. I've never seen her so upset before. I'm happy that Logan simply took him away without arguing with her about it, too."

He got into bed with Londyn and held her

to him. She continued to ask him questions, mostly about his other half as well as the others. He was going to have to let her see his gorilla soon so she'd know how to tell him from his family. Also, he didn't want her to freak out—words that he'd never say to her face if he had to shift to save them. She was yawning when she said something that he'd not heard from his family.

"The Crowns are wanting Allen back, did you hear? They're saying that your family pressured them into letting him go." She snuggled down in the pillow. "Hazel is having a fit, and you can imagine how Jayden is taking it."

When she was asleep, he reached out to his brother. Yes, the couple, Daisy Crown and David Winehouse, were wanting their child back and were in the process of suing Jayden for his and Hazel's part in the kidnapping of their little boy.

"What's going to happen to him? Or you guys, for that matter?" Jayden said that Hazel was, of course, upset and that he was trying his best not to hunt the kids down and beat their asses. "They more than likely heard that there was money, and they're out to get a piece of it."

"That's what Mom said, too. She was a bit

more colorful about it, however. But you're on the right track. They're suing us and Sister Mary Grace. She's one of the sisters at the hospital who helps with the babies. Also, the hospital." He asked him why. "As I said, I don't know, but Mom and Dad are over here tonight getting some loving in. Hazel is beside herself with fear. Logan keeps telling her that they don't have a leg to stand on, but we both know that anything could change at any moment." He did know that and told him he'd be here for him. After thanking him, the two of them closed the connection, and he willed his body to sleep.

Waylon had a truck coming in tomorrow. Mr. Brown's attorney wanted to speak to him as well as he wanted to spend the entire day with Londyn to get to know her better. He just wished they'd have a sort of normal day.

~*~

Sherman tried his best to listen to what was going on with his grandson, but all he could think about was that someone was going to come and take him away from them. Allen was a huge part of him feeling like a new man, and he wasn't willing to give that up easily. Jamie snapped his fingers in front of his face, and he glared at the man.

"I've been saying your name for the last five minutes. I didn't mean to be rude just now, but I was actually concerned that you were having a heart attack." He shook his body, telling the younger man that he was upset. "I understand that too. But I've been looking into things. It's amazing what a person can do when they have so many people willing to do their bidding. But I have it on good authority that Jayden nor Hazel had any contact with the Crown/Winehouse couple."

"What does that have to do with the price of tea in China, might I ask?" Jamie grinned, telling him that was an old saying. "It works, doesn't it? Stop teasing this old man and tell me what it is you're going on about."

"They're claiming that Jayden and Hazel came to the hospital to talk them into letting them have the baby for a price and that they'd not received any money. They've never met. Also there was never a time when there was supposed to be money exchanged for the child. Did you know that they have videos all over the hospital that are simply for the use of things like this one? I didn't. But I'm glad that they did. The hospital is saying that Daisy, the biological mother, got into a huge fight with Sister Mary Grace about her not ever wanting to see the child. The Sister was explaining to her at the time that it was a closed adoption. They'd not know who was taking their unwanted child. We're still trying to figure out how they knew it was this family that adopted him." Sherman said it was more than likely a greedy nurse or someone who had a grudge against one of his grandchildren. "It could very well be. Or their grasping at straws." Jamie looked around, and so did Sherman. "I don't suppose you have any more of those wonderful cookies I had the last time I was here? They were blueberry lemon cookies. I could eat them forever."

After pulling out the little tin that he'd been using as a sewing box for nearly twenty years, he laughed at the look of disappointment on his face. Giving him the cookie jar, he was still laughing when he got up to get the two of them a glass of milk. They were just waiting on the rest of the family to show up, and Sherman decided that he was going to get him a bit of information now before the rest of them came in and started hogging up all the time.

"Something else I want to share with you

while I'm thinking about it. If you'd not mind reminding me when they get here, I'll get around to telling them about Roman Davis as well. He's going to skip a trial and go directly to prison. When he threatened Waylon's wife, who I love like my sister, he threatened me as well. I know that it might not stick, but that's what was on the report. He's also been stripped of his licenses as well. I'm to understand that he had a wholesaler's license as well as having his driver's license." He asked about the man's family. "Mr. Davis is closing down his offices and retiring. That was his idea, not mine. But he said he'd not have to answer awkward questions when people would come around asking them."

"I'll remind you. I don't want to be insensitive here, but have you heard any more about your mother? I know that she's passed on and all but what are the press saying about it? And I want you to know that in no way was I trying to open old wounds." He told him that he'd not heard a whimper of news anywhere. She was just gone. "Good riddance to her, too, if you ask me."

Jamie and Amy's mother had an unhealthy obsession with her son. She thought, even though she was in her late fifties at the time, that she was going to marry her son and have his perfect children. And that they'd be in the White House forever. She'd been killed just recently when she killed two guards while trying to get to her son because she felt that he wasn't getting her messages about being with him. She was a sick individual.

When the family started showing up he was thrilled to see that they brought him little Allen. He loved that little boy more than he could explain to someone and was happiest when he could hold him and feed him his bottle. The little tyke looked at him, too, like he knew that the two of them were going to be up to no good before too much longer.

There was food aplenty, too. Sherman loved pizza. His favorite thing of all time was one of them calzone meatball subs. He could nearly eat an entire one all by himself. Of course, he didn't, having to share with the rest of the family, but he was happy when there were leftovers. A cold meatball sammich was about the best there was over a hot one.

Jamie, true to his word, had to have him remind him of the things they'd talked about. Sherman loved having to be the one that kept the younger man in line. It did his heart good, too, to see him getting along with his family, too. The man even changed a nasty diaper like it was nothing to him. He supposed it was.

After all the food mess was cleaned up, he was given another bottle to feed young Allen. Since he'd already heard about the things that Jamie had to say, he was content to sit in the library and rock his great-grandson to sleep. He might well have dozed off a few times as well, but he was forever careful that he didn't get too deep in sleep so he'd not drop the little man.

Londyn came into the room just as Allen was fussing about his diaper and he asked her if she had any practice in changing him. After telling him that she did, she had his diaper off and a clean one on him before he could put up a fuss about taking the little baby away.

"I have something I'd like to ask you." He figured that she'd want to talk to one of the others, telling her that he was an old man and that he didn't know all that much anymore. "I don't think that's the slightest bit true. I think, no, I know you can run circles around everyone in this house and they'd not know what happened if you were to put your mind to something. But this is important to me."

"All right, darling, you go on ahead and tell me, and between the two of us, we'll get it all worked out." She paced a bit, and he let her. Jayden came in to get the baby and while he was sorry to see him go, he was kind of glad for it. He was going to get to be the knight for Londyn so he wanted to pay attention to what she had to say to him. "Are you sure you want to ask me?"

"I'm sure. I have some money now. A lot more than I ever expected to have in my lifetime. But I lost my family in order to get it." He nodded, hearing about how her family were all killed in a landslide. "I want your help in setting up a fund to help people get the kind of information that I should have used for my own family. Like how to find out where their insurance records might be. What kind of things need to be put in a will. Getting cemetery and services paid for in advance. I don't want to do that sort of work. I think that might be something later down the road, but that's something that I think everyone could use."

"I didn't have mine worked out until a few years ago. We were going to be buried in the same church cemetery that we got married in. A nice bit of land out there that has a pretty little cherry tree by it. I'd love to be there, looking up at the blooms and think of the day we got married. That's what I was thinking. Now we're all going to be living forever, and I don't know that I'll ever be put into that hole and swallowed up." He looked up at her. "You'd come and visit me, wouldn't you, darling? I sure would like that."

"I don't want to think about you being swallowed up, thank you. You're my grandda since I have none to claim as my own. And I would surely visit you if it came to that. You're the glue that holds this family together. Did you know that? I've heard them all say that they're going to go to Grandpa Sherman for advice at least a dozen times in the last week or so."

"Oh, go on with you. Glue? Well, I do try and keep the peace." He didn't, and she was sure that they both knew that. He loved to pick at the boys just to get them going on each other. It made his day to have them get all huffy with their brothers. "I tell you what. I'll put together a list of things, and you and I will work on it. Yes, sir. That's something that I'd love to do with my favorite granddaughter."

"We're all your favorites, and you know it." When she kissed him on the forehead, he felt blessed. For a man to have so many people loving him, Sherman thought that he was about as lucky as anyone could be right now.

Chapter 5

Trying not to overwhelm her, Waylon let his gorilla reach out and touch her gently. He'd never had a relationship with his other half like his brothers. They said they controlled him. But Waylon's gorilla seemed to know when he was in his place that he was in control. He could ask him to be easy, but usually, he did what he wanted.

"Do you have a name for him?" No one had ever asked him that before, and he was surprised that she understood that they were two different people. After telling her what he called himself, she laughed. "I guess that he feels like he could be called anything that he liked, but that's perfect. Hello Brutis. My name is Londyn Dixon."

"*Tell her that I know her name.*" Waylon laughed when his beast sounded like a petulant child. "*I'm not a child either.*"

"I can understand him." They both looked at Londyn, and he thought that his beast was more surprised than he was. "You're very handsome, aren't you? And bigger than I thought you'd be."

"I am his beast. I care for him when he needs it." The voice in his head was strong, and it occurred to him that he didn't know what language he was speaking in, nor for that matter if he was talking a language that only he could understand with Londyn and his beast.

"Why do you call him that? Or yourself? Why do you call yourself beast when you seem like any other gorilla, with the exception of size, something that sounds so terrifying?" It was Burtis who answered her. "I guess I can see that. If people think that you refer to him as that then they'll think twice about attacking. Have you hurt anyone in order to protect Waylon?"

"I have only harmed those that think to harm him." She seemed to be satisfied with that answer. As she walked around him, touching his great other half, he began to look around to see what other things he might have missed being a man. *"Our mate is very strong, isn't she? And smart."*

"I believe that she's both of those things, yes. She's looking for a job. I worry about that because I can't be with her all the time. I fear that she'll be hurt

while I'm too far away to come and help her." Brutis laughed and told him that he shouldn't fear that she couldn't protect herself. *"Do you think that she'll be able to defend herself all the time? Against all odds?"*

"Nay. What I think is that she won't allow herself to get into a situation that is that far over her boundaries. She is very self-aware. Just look at how she is looking at us and also the surrounding area. She will not allow any of us to be harmed if she can help it. Also, I believe that she will be a good mother to your children. Protective, of course, but she will teach them to be strong and smart as well." Now that it was pointed out to him, he could see that she wasn't just looking at his other half, but just as he'd been told, she was keeping track of her surroundings. It was just one more thing to love about her.

They hung out in the yard for another hour. When Brutis laid down on the soft grass, she curled up into his body and fell asleep. Brutis and he both thought that they could live with her right there for the rest of their long lives. It was comforting to them both that she trusted them completely.

When she woke up, he'd been trying to move out from under her when he got a leg cramp. She looked up at him. With her smile, brightening up the world it seemed looking at him, Waylon realized that he loved her more than he did yesterday and would love her all the more tomorrow.

It wasn't a surprise to him that she was sleeping a great deal of the time. They were up most of the night making love and enjoying being together. Just this morning, he'd joined her in the shower to have a nice little romp in the water, and both of them had to stagger their way to the bed again for a quick nap. If they kept this up, they were going to be worn to a nubbin. Whatever the hell that was. Just thinking about her had him hard. And when he shifted back to himself, his human side, he was thrilled that she was as hungry as he was in needing some dinner.

They'd been so busy with other things going on, he was gearing up for the holidays in the hardware store with extras coming in, and she was busy establishing herself as an attorney who worked solely for the family.

He and Berny, his employee, were working to get most of the truck put away when the younger man came to find him. They were nearly finished with it but still had some of the end of summer things to put on clearance. The herbs that he'd sold this summer had been a big hit, and he was going to do that again next year. Maybe bring in a few trees to help with the refurbishing of the trees that had been damaged when the summer storms came through earlier in the year.

"Mr. Waylon? I was wondering if you have the Thanksgiving schedule fixed up yet. I know it's a few months away but my mom is biting at the bit in trying to gather all of us up for the holiday. I have five brothers and three sisters and most of them have their own families. I'd rather work, to be honest, but my mom would have a fit if I had to." He told him that he could have off any day that he needed to be with his family. "Gee, thanks. I'll tell her."

Waylon found himself laughing throughout the day when he thought about how Berny had seemed to be dejected about Thanksgiving with his family. It got him to thinking about his own plans for this year now that he had a mate. He checked his pocket again for the ring that he'd gotten her yesterday and had it sized so that he could pick it up today. He was as excited about giving it to her as Berney wasn't about his own family plans.

"*I have a question for you. More like a favor, I guess.*" He smiled when Cullen spoke to him. "*I have to go out of town for a few days. Can I count on you to keep up with the people working on the house that I'm having renovated for Logan? He said that he needs his own space, and I do as well. I'm not used to having people around sharing my space all the time.*"

"*Who's doing the renovations?*" He told him that Amy's company was. "*Good. Yes, I'd love to help you out with that. Are you looking for a house of your own right now? I mean, your mate has to be out there.*"

There was silence then. Not sure if he hurt his brother or not, he was ready to tell him how sorry he was when he spoke again. Whatever he expected him to say, he was positive that him telling him that he'd rather not have a mate because of the things that he'd done was not it.

"*I don't believe that she'll care, Cullen.*" He told him that he would. "*I also don't think that it works like that. When she comes to you, and I'm sure that she will, she'll be able to be a part of you that you never expected.*"

"*What if I'm too much for her. I know that I am to myself all the time. The nightmares are enough to make me wake up in a cold sweat. And I don't know if I do or not, but I think that I scream myself awake when I have them. No one is going to put up with that in someone who is supposed to be loving and kind to me. I'm not very loveable in the event you never saw that."* For some reason, that made him laugh. *"I really have no idea why you'd think that was funny, but I'm going to let it go for now. I have to go out tonight, and I should be back sometime on Wednesday. That's three days from now. Don't tell Mom and Dad that I'm going out, please?"*

"I can't lie to them any more than you could." He asked him to avoid them then. *"That might be difficult as well. When they get it out of me, what is it you want me to say? I need to have some information."*

"I'm going to be on duty." That was all he said, and while it wasn't enough, he figured that he wasn't going to get any more from his little brother. *"I hate that I have to do this, but it's important to a great many people. I've made you the power of attorney, by the way if something should happen to me. I know that we're all immortal, but there are still things that could happen that would make it so that I'd not want to be around."*

"You're scaring me a bit, Cullen. What is it that

you're doing so that if I see it on the news, I'm not going to jump to conclusions." He said it would never be on the news as it was going to be an in and out situation. *"I don't like this. I'm sure you don't either but I really don't like that you're going in to work when you're supposed to be recuperating at home."*

"I don't like it either, but I'm the only one that can take care of this. Don't call Jamie either. The very fact that he called me in is going to piss off a great many people in this family. Also, I wanted to tell you something that I don't say often enough. I love you, Waylon. All of you guys. And while everyone thinks that I'm closest to Dallas, you're the one that I have the most faith in to get things done for me."

He felt his eyes fill with tears and had to wipe them twice before he could speak again. It was too late then; Cullen had closed the connection and now he was left wondering what he'd do if something were to happen to him.

Cullen had always been the baby in the family, but after he was about sixteen, he began taking on roles that made him seem so much wiser than his years. He always had a job. And when he was working, he did the best that he could for whatever he was working on. A good work ethic wasn't just something that he did. Cullen lived by it.

All of them had good work ethics. Even though they hadn't been born rich, he thought that had a great deal to do with it. They all worked for a living, too. Money, his grandda told him, didn't grow on trees, and they were some of the lucky ones in that they didn't have to worry about money but that they should anyway. They all lived by that rule.

After Berny left for the day, he decided that he'd had enough fun for one day and was just closing up when someone, a fairly young couple, walked into the store. He didn't know them and figured that they were from out of town when the girl came up to the counter looking at him like he'd done her wrong or something.

"Are you the one that has my son?" He knew immediately who they were but didn't say anything to her question. "I want him back. My parents are making it hard on me to see my boyfriend, and I want to just move out. I heard that you can get more food stamps if you have a baby. So bring him here, and I won't have to press charges against you for kidnapping. You told me to give him up, and I didn't want to."

Waylon reached out to his entire family and let them know what was going on. It was Dallas who said he was the closet, and he said he'd be there in a few minutes. The girl asked him if he was stupid or something.

"Not as stupid as you seem to be." The man, really just a boy it looked like to him that hadn't had to change razors in all the time he'd been shaving. There was very little peach fuzz on his face that was covered in zits. "I don't have any idea who you are. Or, for that matter, what it is you're talking about. What baby do you think I have?"

"Mine. You are stupid, aren't you? Bring him here so that I can take him to the welfare office. They'll even give me an apartment that I can live in for free." Not wanting to antagonize her any more than she already was, he kept an eye on the boy/man. "Well? When do I get him?"

When the little bell sounded, he was never so happy to see anyone as he was at that moment. Dallas went to the back of the store where the boy was and struck up a conversation with him. Dealing with the girl as best he could, he told her that he didn't have any children and that he'd only just found someone that he wanted to marry. And that if she wasn't going to buy anything, she really should be on her way.

"I've called the police." Relief so profound raced over his skin. *"You're doing fine. Just keep her talking, and remember, you're immortal, and there are cameras pointing directly at the two of you. It's all going to be just fine."*

"Sure, you're standing back there with the quiet one." He told him that he was the one that was armed. *"Christ. I didn't need to know that."*

Daisy, he thought that was her name, was going on and on about what she was going to get for free once he brought her the baby. Even if she were to shoot him full of holes, he didn't believe for a moment that anyone would give her any child. Not even a doll. She was off her rocker. The slap to his face had him snarling at her, and she finally took a step back and shut her mouth.

"Listen, kid. You come in here spouting off shit that I have nothing to do with. But I do know that you legally gave up your child. Hell, any idiot could see that was the only smart thing you've ever done for her." He was trying to trip her up, and it worked.

"It's a girl? I guess I don't care so long as I have her back with me. I have shit to do. So when are you going to—" She turned when the bell rang. Then looked at him like he'd offended her in some way. "You couldn't have called the cops. What the hell are they doing here?"

"You assaulted me." Rollin asked her to come outside, and she, of course, refused. When he told her that she was going to be arrested for trespassing, she turned and glared at him. Waylon just laughed. "Get her out of here, and yes, I'll press charges for her hitting me. Not to mention accusing me of taking her child. Which, by the way, she hasn't any idea what it is."

Once they were gone, Dallas came up to the counter with young David, his name only just then coming to him. Wondering what was going on, he laid the gun he had on the countertop and said that he'd never have shot him. That he didn't want the kid to come back as he was better off without Daisy.

"Smart man." He nodded and was taken away in the second cruiser. "What are your plans when this is all over?"

"Run away. She's been making me do stuff

for her since we were kids in second grade. I need to get away from her before she makes me end up in prison." Dallas told Rollin that he was going to take care that David was in good hands and took him outside to the front of the store.

He didn't have any doubt that by the end of their conversation that David would have enough money to get out of town and have a job lined up for him when he got there.

After closing up and going to the station house, he did the necessary paperwork to have her out of his hair and went home. There were more important things to do there than anything that he might have had going on at work.

~*~

Not having any idea how to initiate sex, Londyn decided to just meet him at the door and be done with it. That did sound better when she was only thinking about sex, to her. They'd been making love all night long for the past two weeks, and she wanted to have sex, then fall into a deep sleep and not wake up until her body was really rested. Of course, she did that after sex in the middle of the night as well as in the morning, but she was needy now and didn't want to wait on him.

She decided that she was thinking of this all wrong and wanted to just forget it. To think that she wanted to have sex so that she could be relaxed enough to sleep. Her mind was all fuzzy with stupid thoughts today. Not to mention, she had the worst kind of headache she'd ever had, too.

When he came into the door, she could tell that he was stressed out as well. Telling herself to think about this as a sign that he was just as stressed out as well, she let go of her plans to seduce him. As soon as they were alone in the living room, her sitting next to him, he got down in front of her and pulled out a little box. Her heart started pounding the moment that he smiled at her.

"Will you marry me?" He laughed with her. "I could get all sappy about it, but I don't think you're that kind of woman. I've discovered that I don't want to go on living like we are and would very much like to have you legally bound to me. Just in case you meet someone else."

"That has been my thinking all along." Waylon tickled her. "Don't. You'll make me pee myself. But go on, be non-sappy when you ask me to marry you. By the way, I'm going to say yes. I don't want you to change your mind and say fuck it after you asked me already."

"I love you so much, Londyn. I want to have children with you. I want to be the first thing you think of in the morning and the last at night. You are my all, and if you left me, I don't know what I'd do with myself." She told him she loved him too and would never leave him. "I'm so happy to hear that."

Once he slipped the ring on her finger, she got a good look at it. He told her that the stones were blue diamonds surrounding a purple amethyst. The wide band had their names on the inside of it, and it was polished to a high gleam. When it sparkled over the walls in the room, she had a thought that a Christmas tree was going to be best looking in this room by the window. So it could shine and shine around the room as well.

Kissing him, she made her way down to his ear lobe. She found it incredibly warming to have him suckle at hers and wanted to see if it did the same for him. At his low growl, she moved along his throat.

Londyn bit his skin as gently as she could and felt the pounding of his pulse as she licked over the engorged vein. His hands slid up under her skirt, and she felt him slide his fingers deep into her. That was just what she needed. Him right here for her.

Reaching between them, she cupped his cock. Christ, she wanted him right fucking now and lifted her head to tell him. But he pulled away, and she nearly fell back over onto the couch. Things went from them just kissing over their engagement to fast and dirty sex, again, something that she dearly needed.

Leaning back, Waylon tore at his pants, and she watched as he freed his cock. When she reached for him and wrapped her hands around him, he groaned. Before she could taste him, he picked her up by her ass again and took them to the floor. Her breath caught when she felt him riding her through her clothing.

"I need to be in you." She nodded as he pulled her skirt up over her hips. "Christ, I've never wanted you this badly before. It's like I've never had you before, and I need to claim you again."

He tore her panties from her and moved to her entrance. When he hesitated, she pulled him down to her mouth and kissed him. As soon as he slammed into her, she pressed her mouth over his left nipple and suckled as hard as she could while playing with the tight nipple at his chest.

Pain seared through her, and she cried out against his throat. It wasn't painful, not like the first time they'd had sex, but it was still an intrusion that she wasn't prepared for just then. When he started to lift off her, she wrapped her legs around him and felt his cock jerk inside of her.

Waylon moved slowly now. The pain of his large thick cock was now being replaced by the most incredible pleasure. She knew what was building, knew that her own release was close, and she sealed the wound she'd not realized that she'd made on his nipple by licking over it with her tongue and moaning when he pinched her nipple through her bra and blouse.

"Come for me. I want...no Christ, I need for you to come." He tore the buttons opened and shifted her bra down over her breast as he sank his teeth into her nipple. Even as he fucked her, he reached down and tilted her ass upward, and she came apart.

The climax took her breath away, and she

would swear forever that her heart stopped beating for a long few seconds while she adjusted to this new high with him. Christ, she felt like she could go to the moon and back on the pleasure of it all.

Crying out, he lifted his head. His command for her to come again brought her to climax, and his body stiffened above her as he joined her. She pulled him down and sank her canines into his pounding pulse as he filled her.

Londyn felt his second climax even as his first finished. Lifting her head from his throat, she pulled off her bra and fed it to him, wondering as she did what she was doing. Then his mouth took her, and she cried out again, a climax that rolled over her like a warm summer storm.

He stiffened above her, and all she could think about was his beast and how much they indeed looked alike. Acted like each other as well. She could see him then. His beast, just enough of him that she knew that the two of them would always protect her, but most of all, they would love her no matter what.

Waylon dropped down atop her, but not with all his weight. Turning at the last moment, he rolled to his back, taking her with him. His cock, semi-hard, she could feel it still inside of her. And every time that it twitched, even just a little, she felt herself have just one more climax. Her body was worn down, out for the count, and she never wanted to move again.

When she woke up, not only was she in bed, but she was alone in it. Moving her hand to his pillow to see how long he'd been gone. It was still warm and she noticed that the bathroom light was on from beneath the door. When he stepped out, turning off the light immediately, she opened up the covers, and he got in beside her. After the warm bed, he was too chilly to be snuggling up against her, but she loved him, so she allowed it.

"I nearly dropped you several times while carrying you up here. You're not at all heavy, but I was weak-kneed and needed a nap." She thanked him for not just putting her on the steps and leaving her. "Yeah, the staff would have been freaked out, I think."

They both laughed, and he put his cold feet on her leg. "That's not nice. What am I going to do with you when it's winter outside? Toss you out of the bed? I should make you wear socks to bed."

"I can't. I have nightmares." He was finally

beginning to warm up, and she felt better. After a few more minutes, she was nearly asleep again when he spoke in the darkness. "Daisy has been cited for trespassing at the store, as I told you. She's pissed off now that she's unable to get in touch with David too. His parents disowned him. Did I tell you that?"

"I don't understand people like that. What do they expect to do now? He's barely nineteen, I heard somewhere. I guess, too, though it's good that he's getting away from Daisy. She sounds like a fruit." He laughed when she laid back down. "You said that Dallas helped him get away. I'm assuming that he knows something about the boy more than you do."

"He said that his desire was to go to college but he didn't think that he could ever afford it. And he was really upset that Daisy had him by the hook about the baby. He's not even sure that it's his." She asked if he wanted anything to do with it. Even now. "No. He thinks that the child will be better off where he is and out of their lives. Dallas has set him up with a job and a couple that he'll be living with. They'll keep him towing the line, and he should be all right." She hoped so.

The next time she woke up, the sun was high in the sky, and the bed on Waylon's side was cold. Getting up, she noticed that the shower was dry and figured that he'd been up and gone for a while. Taking her time in the shower, new sore places on her body, she was dressed and downstairs when she looked at her phone.

"Oh shit." It was nearly one in the afternoon. She'd never slept that late in her life. Glad that she was going to be getting some work done despite her getting going so late, Londyn asked for burgers on the grill tonight with some French fries. She was going to test out that saying that she couldn't gain any weight married to Waylon. Right now she thought she could eat her weight through a large bag of chips and dip.

Getting in her new car, one that she'd picked up just yesterday, she made her way to the store. It wasn't much of one, and she knew that she'd have to go to a bigger one in Coshocton, but for now, she could pick up some salad fixings for dinner as well as some much-needed fruit. Her love of anything fresh was all she craved anymore, and she hoped that she could get some baby carrots to much on. Otherwise, she really was going to be as big as a house, no matter what the saying said.

After getting everything she needed at the store, she was headed out again when she saw Falkner kneeling down on the ground with a little girl crying. Picking up her purse, forever with a first aid kit on her, she asked if he needed any help. After a quick smile at her, he told her what was going on.

"Besty here thought that she could climb the tree higher than her brother could. Paul is fourteen to her eight. I told her the next time she wanted to climb a tree, make sure that it was close to home. That way, if she fell out of it, her mommy could find her. As it is now, her mother called the police when her daughter came up missing. She's on her way here now.

The woman came to a screeching halt where they were on the sidewalk. She leapt out of the car before it was turned off and had to retrace her steps to do that. She was terrified, and it showed all over her face. After helping get the little one to the car, she asked Falkner if he wanted to get a quick drink with her, and he said he'd never turn down a date with a beautiful woman.

Sitting at one of the many picnic tables

around the Dari Twist, the two of them talked about the weather and anything else they wanted. She loved this family more and more by spending just a little bit of time with them. It was great having a family.

Chapter 6

Booth was glad for the time to spend with his brothers. Even though three of them had their mates, they still carved out time for them to be brothers again. They were just being served their salads, a big part of their meal, when a man with several armed what appeared to be guards came into their little section of the restaurant and asked for a Mr. Dixon.

And being the smart asses they were, they all six said yes, that was who they were. The man looked about as flustered as he seemed to be pissed off, which wasn't saying much. He looked to be always pissed off. Then, with a short nod, the armed men stepped around them all and stood with their hands on their weapons. Their faces couldn't be seen, but it was apparent who was in charge of whatever was going on. The man just so happened to be standing in front of him when he demanded to speak to the idiot who was teaching kids how to speak other languages. Again, the six of them said yes, it was them.

"For Christ's sake. This person's name is Booth. Booth Dixon. I want him to come with me right now so that I can get out of this small town and back to my own office." Booth stood up, and he looked at the others. "Was that so hard? Christ, you small-town idiots really burn my ass. Let's go, young man. I have a deadline to meet, and you've wasted enough of my time with your little games."

"I'm Booth Dixon, but I'm not going anywhere with you. And to call us idiots when it's obvious that we can speak more languages than you or you'd not need us. Isn't that about right?" He asked him if he wanted to be arrested. "For being Booth? I don't think so. Besides that, you might want to take a look around, buster. My brothers have taken exception to your treatment of me."

"That's it. I've had—arrest this man. He's not cooperating with his government when they need him." No one moved, not even the men that were directly behind him. It was then that the man turned around and saw that Waylon and the others, with the exception of Dallas had shifted and were now holding the head of each man in their large hands that were right in front of them. "What the hell is the meaning of this? You will… how did you bring these monkeys in here?"

"We're apes, not monkeys. Actually, we're great apes. Now, as I was saying, I'm not going anywhere with you. You're rude and a straight-up bastard. But that's not the real reason. I don't like you. We were having a great time, and I can't believe that you've come in here with your armed men. Well, they were armed and thought to fuck up our day." He reached out to Amy and told her what was going on and could she please call her brother. "What the hell is your name anyway?"

"None of your business." Booth sat down and then heard from Amy. She told him that he had nothing to worry about. While the man was going on and on about what he was going to be doing if he allowed him to while he spoke to his sister-in-law.

"His name is Alexander Winterson. He works for the government, that's true but he's only looking for you because Jamie suggested that he ask you about translating some papers that were found in an abandoned house in DC. He said that was all he did

was suggest that you might be able to or know someone who can help out. I don't know anything about that other than Jamie is pissed off because of the tactics that Winterson is using." He said that he'd caused them all to shift, and the only ones that weren't were him and Dallas. *"He'd shit his pants if one of you were to go all apeshit on them, don't you think? I'm going to suggest it to one of them now."*

She must have said something to Dallas because, in no time at all, Waylon stood up on his feet and pounded on his chest like they had seen in the movies. Each of the soldiers that were with Winterson not only dropped their weapons but dropped to the floor along with their hands over their heads. It looked like all their bravery was gone now. They were, it looked like they were smart in this, terrified. In the silence of the room, a cell phone rang.

Dallas pulled out his phone and put it in front of Winterson. "It's for you." The man didn't look like he was going to take it. Just then, everyone in the room who had a cell found it to be ringing. It was the most comical thing he'd ever seen. "I'd answer that if I were you. It could be the difference between you living and dying right here on the floor. I was told not to hurt you unless you provoked me, and I can tell you right now that you're very close to being on my last fucking nerve."

Winterson snatched the phone from Dallas and put it up to his ear after connecting. All he got out was 'who is' before he paled a little and began sputtering about how it was his fault that things had gone awry. His glare at him was something that he'd not expected like he was blaming him for whomever he was speaking to.

When he hung up he stood there looking like he'd just lost his best friend and lost the girl too. When he straightened out his tie and handed the phone back to Dallas, he looked like he was at a loss for words up until he found them.

"You actually called the president of these United States on me? I hope you know that his little tantrum didn't do anything to me. You'd best bet that I'm going to come out smelling like a rose while you smell like the shit that you are." He told him that he was bothering him. "Now he, the stupid shit that we have as a president, wants me to come home and count my blessings that he's not fired me. For doing my job. Can you believe that? You'll pay for this, see that you don't. I swear you'd better be watching yourself from now on. I'm going to be keeping an eye on you. See that I don't."

"You didn't learn anything from this, did you?" Winterson asked Booth what he was supposed to have learned. "That you're a bastard and a bully and just got your ass handed to you by your own boss didn't mean a thing to you. I'm sure that he told you how wrong you were in treating someone you need a favor from to be nicer to."

"You're still going to do as you're told. And coming with me to get those papers translated will be your only job from now on. I don't give a rat's ass what that man said to me. When I'm given an assignment, I take it on with full guns." Booth just shook his head. "Get your gear gathered up, and we'll be on our way. I believe that we've wasted enough time on your poor little feelings for one day."

Booth didn't move. But the men that came with Winterson had simply gathered up their weapons and left the man standing alone. Waylon stayed his gorilla, and it made him wonder when was the last time that he had himself a good run.

Or even slept out under the stars as they used to do as kids. It was going to be something that he—

"Did you hear me?" Booth asked him if he'd heard what he said. "I don't like that you're not doing what I want. Get your ass in gear, and let's be on our way. I have things to do, and hanging out with a panty waste like you is getting nothing done. Get up. Right now or so help me, you're going to be shot in the head."

"Don't shoot my brother. You'll only serve to piss him off." Just as he was reaching into his suit pocket it was Cullen that disarmed him. The gun fell to the floor, and then Winterson was there as well. Cullen had him not just in a good tight grip but he also was making it difficult for him to breathe as well. "Remember Cullen, he's human."

"Yeah, I guess he might be considered a non-shifter, but there is no way that I'd call him human. He's been like this his entire life, too." When Cullen didn't explain what that meant, he asked him. "He bullied his parents, too, and his sister until they didn't want to have anything to do with him. He'd been a pain in the ass for some time to the president as well."

Winterson looked like he wanted to speak,

but his brother only gave him enough breath to breathe for a bit longer. Cullen didn't seem all that impressed either that the man was someone who was working for the president. He did, too, he supposed, but there was something more going on here than just what they were dealing with at the moment. When his cell rang, he answered it without looking to see who it might well be.

"Booth, I'm assuming." He said that it was him. "This is Jamie. I was wondering if the idiot had ever apologized to you." He told him what was going on. "I see. So, I'm going to assume that's a no. All right. If you'll allow me to speak to one of the…are the secret service still there?"

He handed his phone to the man on the floor, who said that he was in charge. Not saying much on his end, none of them seemed to have any idea why the man simply stood up and put his gun to the back of Winterson's head. Booth was sure that things were going to get shitty here in a few minutes when, all of a sudden, the room filled with police as well as other agents. Then the phone was handed back to him.

"Booth, I'm so sorry this has happened to you. And your brothers, I was told you were just having a nice get-together when Winterson came in spouting his gibberish. I swear the man has gotten on my last nerve over the past two weeks. I believe he's part of the people that were out to get my wife and myself killed a few weeks back." He told him he was sorry about that but that the police were there as well as the other. "Yes, they're going to be getting him out of your hair and into a nice quiet jail someplace until I have time to fuss with him. Which might be a few years for the way I'm feeling right now."

"What did he want? Something about translating something for you." He told him not to worry about it now. He'd find someone else to take care of it. "I don't mind. I'm off school right now with it being summer break and would love to look over the paperwork for you."

"Really? You would save me so much time, Booth. I haven't any idea what the paperwork might entail. There has been speculation that it's just a simple recipe but I don't speak whatever the language is that it's written in." He told the other man that he was fluent in several languages but if it was something that he didn't know, he had friends that could help out. "I'll have to know who they are before you send it to them. Like I said, it looks like a recipe but it's difficult to know what it is. I'll have them couriered over to you as soon as today. Whatever you need, just tell me, and I'll get it for you.

By the time the room was cleaned out but for the six of them, the night seemed to have been ruined. They were, however, going to go on a nice run through woods and climb a few trees while they were at it. It was, after all the things that had happened in the last few weeks, nice to be able to just be their other selves for a change. He knew that it was for him.

It was nearly midnight when he made it back to his place. The courier was there waiting for him to sign for the thick envelope, and he felt bad about that. Taking it into the house, he didn't bother opening it up because he knew that he'd get involved in it, and that would be the end of his good night's sleep.

As soon as he got into bed, Booth knew that it was a lost cause. He lay there tossing and turning, wondering what the papers said. Getting up and taking another shower to get himself in the mood, he was sitting at his desk looking over the first few sheets of paper and realized that it was a recipe. One for baked brie. He hoped that the rest of the papers were that easy but he knew better than to think that. As soon as he got to the second page, it was written out how the allies, the United States, were sending troops to the fort to fight on night maneuvers.

At six in the morning, he was picking up his phone when it rang before he could touch it. It was Jamie again. He wanted to know when he was going to start working on them, and he also wanted him to keep track of his hours. After telling him what the first page was about, he told him what a wonderful find the paperwork had been about the Civil War and some of the maneuvers that had been launched in order to get their freedom.

"It reads like someone was just jotting down their thoughts. There are also references to how much money was being spent and on what sort of goods. This is wonderful so far, and I'm really enjoying myself." After telling him how far he'd gotten and the things that he'd found out, Jamie wanted him to come to DC to read it to him. He was also a history buff and wanted to hear the accountings as he was reading them. "There is a whole passage on how the person writing this met Lincoln. He said that he was a good man but tall. He mentions that several times in the first couple of pages." He asked him where the papers were found.

"It's a long-dead relative of Edwin Staton. He was a former U.S. Attorney General back then, and he had some far distant cousins that he might have stayed with while in the DC area. The house had been abandoned for some time, and when it went on the market, the new owners were doing some remodeling, bringing it up to code. I was told when they tore open a wall and found this little room with things like that you're reading in it. There are books as well that are going to be donated to the library." He asked him what the people who owned the house thought about that. "The realtor told them that the house was just old enough that it might have national treasures in it that they had to turn over to the government. I don't think that it was legal him telling them that but they were more than pleased to be able to impart some history with their home."

They talked for another thirty minutes when Jamie had to go to some meetings. After talking to him about the papers, he went back to the first page and began taking notes on what was being said. He was especially excited about the recipe then, to know that it was a part of the history of an old house in DC.

~*~

Lydia, Dee, to her friends, didn't like driving in DC. It was difficult to get around and she was sure that every other street was named something to do with a senator or something. And there were so many round abouts that she never knew where to get off. Give her an old-fashioned stoplight, and she'd be just as happy.

The man behind her in traffic had been tailing her for the last hour. After pulling out into traffic a few streets back, he'd been screaming obscenities at her at every stop sign and light. She wasn't going fast enough, he kept telling her, but she wouldn't speed up for anyone. It was against the law and she couldn't afford a ticket right now.

Stopped at a light with him behind her, she kept both her hands on the wheel when he continued to yell and rev up his engines. Like that would be something that would frighten her into speeding through a red light. Then she started moving.

He was pushing her into the oncoming traffic, and she was suddenly afraid. Once she was in the middle of the road, barely missing several cars coming toward her, she was hit in the side. After the airbags were deployed, she felt herself being tossed around like a ball in a dryer and couldn't make heads or tails of where she was or what was going on.

"Miss? Can you hear me?" She tried to open her eyes to look to where the voice was coming from and she couldn't make them work. "Do you know your name, miss? Can you tell me who you are?"

"Lydia Townhouse. My friends call me Dee." She was starting to get her bearings then and asked the man where she was. "That man, the one behind me, he pushed me into oncoming traffic. I want to press charges against him."

"The police will want to talk to you about that, I guess. I'm here to try and get you out of your car." She said that she could unlock it. "I'm afraid we're well beyond that point, honey. You're penned in and upside down. You took quite a beating with your car."

By the time they were able to get the doors off her car and were pulling her out, she began to take inventory of her body, and nothing seemed to be in pain. Even them helping her out with a gurney to the awaiting ambulance had her wondering how it was that she'd been in an accident. She was trying her best to be nice. It wasn't their fault that she'd been hurt. She was ready to throw up or be knocked out. Her head was hurting her so bad that she was surprised that she could even think, much less answer their questions. Almost as soon as she was in the back of the ambulance, there was a pinch to her arm and she was feeling better. She did, however, get a good look at the intersection she'd been at the light at.

There were cars everywhere, it seemed. Right there in the middle of it was a large helicopter. She didn't know if it was any bigger than any other one, but it looked huge to her when they were. They were telling her that she'd be life-flighted to the hospital and that they were ready for her.

She kept floating in and out of consciousness. Dee knew that she had on a neck brace but they kept asking her if she could feel her toes. Trying hard again not to scream at them, she told them that all she felt was pain in her head and that she thought that she was sick with it. Even being drugged up didn't help at all when it came to her being able to answer questions. But the one that kept coming around was the one about her legs.

Closing her eyes once she felt the stabilization of herself, she saw the lights and people in increments of too much light in her eyes. They didn't ask her any more questions, but they did talk around her. At some point, someone did ask her if she had any next of kin and all she could think about was her friend Cullen Dixon. He'd been her best friend since they'd met about ten or so years ago and hadn't been able to be anything more than friends. The date had turned into several over the next few years, and she was forever happy to drop whatever she was doing just to be around the nicest man she'd ever met.

Cullen had been there for her when her dad died. When her cat, older than any other feline that she knew, had passed away in her sleep at the ripe old age of seventeen, he'd seen her through that. She'd been there for him too when he'd come home from being out of the country—all she ever knew about his job and that he might need someone to hang out with and was his sounding board when he would open up about how things were messed up everywhere and that he didn't much care for people, with the exception of her.

He never told her about his big family. She knew that he had one. It had been in all the papers when they'd first met about how this unsung hero was one of six children to his parents and grandparents as well. There was more about him when Amy, sister of Jamie, the president, was found, and since then, there had been plenty of articles about his family that she felt like she could point each of them out and be correct about them.

She wasn't entirely sure if anyone had been able to get in touch with him, but she hoped that he'd not mind that she'd put him as her next of kin, the only person that she truly trusted when she was hurt. Knowing him the way that she did, he'd more than likely tell them to pull the plug, if there had been one, so that she'd not be a bother. Not that she ever was to him, or so he told her, but she loved the big man more than she'd thought possible and not have any sexual thoughts about him.

Waking up once more, just before they were

taking her to surgery, she saw him there. He was her knight in shining armor again and she wanted to sob out her relief. Instead, he leaned over her and kissed her on the cheek. She was never so relived to have a friend with her than she was this friend. He was, and would be forever, her one true friend for life.

"Behave yourself. I don't want to have to go in there and kick your butt simply because you have a break in your spine." She nodded, not entirely sure what he was talking about. "I love you, Dee-Dee."

He was the only person that called her that. The only man who had seen her naked, too. It had been a date, their first one, when she'd spilled wine all over her dress too close to a flame, and both she and the dress caught fire. He jerked her clothing off so quickly that she didn't think a thing about it until later. He took off his jacket and helped her put it on before anyone was the wiser on what had just happened. Dee couldn't believe how many times he'd come to her rescue and never once held it over her head.

Dee swam up from the deep water to be able to see. Someone was talking, not to her, she realized, but talking in the room. Not sure what was going on, only just remembering that she'd been hurt, she tried to pull the things off her face so that she could see, but she couldn't lift her hands up no matter how hard she tried. The hand on face pulled the mask on her face gently but firmly away, and she knew better on some level not to fight.

"You're going to be fine. I have you." She didn't know the voice. Or she didn't know if she knew the voice. Almost as soon as she was told again to behave, she was exhausted and in pain in her head again. "They're giving you something for it now, baby girl. Just let it take you under, and we'll talk when you're awake and feeling better."

Floating away again, she tried to focus on the voice, but it kept fleeting away. Letting the pain medication or whatever it was take effect, she was down again before she could find out if Cullen had left her again.

~*~

"Just how sure are you?" His brother just looked at him with a cocked brow. "I don't mean to question your word, but we've been friends since what seems like forever. And you never mentioned it before."

"I've never met her before now. At least, I don't think so. You've talked about her a great deal, but I don't think that you ever brought her home. What did you say happened? I know you said accident, but I haven't been able to find out anything about it in the papers nor on the news."

"They're trying to keep it hush-hush. The senator who was driving the original truck that pushed her into traffic had a blood alcohol level of .45%. Dee's car was shoved into traffic by him, and eighteen other cars were involved in the accident that she was a tennis ball in. The police are saying that she was hit as many as half a dozen times but other cars, and if not for the men who had pulled her out of the car when it was upside down, there is no telling what she would have had to have done to her when the thing caught fire. As it is now, there are four dead and sixteen injured, three of which aren't expected to live, and the senator is under house arrest and expected to be arrested as soon as tomorrow. Jamie, as you probably have figured out, is looking to have him lynched." Booth asked what he was saying. "That it was her fault. Something about her not getting her ass in gear when she had to know that he was someone important. They're trying to figure out if he was just drunk off his ass or stoned as well. There was enough coke and other paraphernalia in his truck to have felled one of us. Christ, you should have heard him barking orders about Dee when he found out that she'd been brought in by chopper and he'd had to ride here in a police cruiser. He was acting like this was all her fault, too."

Cullen and Booth took turns going in and out of her room. After surgery, she was put on a special floor so that the press couldn't find her nor Senator Fullner. The man was going to be in big-time trouble if he didn't keep his mouth shut and away from the press. To hear him talk about it, there should be special roads for people like him so that he didn't have to deal with John Q. Public when he was late getting around. The man was certifiable.

The room that she was in was private. Even if Jamie hadn't of made sure that she got the best of care, he would have. She was his friend and had been someone that he could cry on her shoulder when he needed it. Right now, she needed him more and he'd not let her down. Also, he'd be there for her when she woke up and found out that she'd never walk again, much less be able to use her arms and body. Cullen wondered if her being mate to his brother Booth would help with that in any way. He hoped so. He wanted to see her dance again.

Their parents showed up around seven the next morning. They were still monitoring her every fifteen minutes and he and Booth could only see her ten minutes at a time each hour. They weren't able to touch her, nor were they able to talk to her if she woke up. He and her had a connection made between them years ago, and he'd speak to her when he wanted and needed to and be damned their rules.

It was Falkner who looked over her chart and told them what the doctors hadn't. She was going to be paralyzed from the waist down because of the accident, and he was hurt all the way to his feet for that. Whether or not Booth could heal her, no one knew just yet. But for now, they were holding off in healing anything about her because of the circumstances of the accident. If she were to heal up too quickly, there would be hell to pay, and he didn't want that for his best buddy.

Chapter 7

Waylon was having so much fun shopping for supplies that he nearly forgot that it was something that he usually hated doing. They were going to do a reset in the hardware store in a few weeks, and there was a need for extra shelving. He was going to have an entire wall filled with things so that construction workers could see what sort of package deals he could do for them. Just as he was looking over the newest in peg boards, his cell phone went off. Answering it with a heavy heart, he wondered why his dad would use a phone rather than just contacting him. The first thing he asked was if everyone was all right.

"Yes, everyone is good. Booth is spending a great deal of time at the hospital, as he should, but other than that, everything is fine. I have a question for you, and I was wondering if you could spare me a few minutes after you get back home." He told his dad that he would make sure he had time for him forever. "Thank you for that, son. I needed to hear that. I have myself a problem that might need your expertise on remodeling the pantry. Just what sort of things I'd need to consider and what not. I know that sounds so mundane, but I want to expand it for the holidays and when you all come over but I don't even know where to begin. I won't be doing the work myself, oh no, I know better than that, but get you to help me find someone other than Amy's crew to do it. I'm hoping that once we get it done up, you or one of your brothers will move into this big old house, and we move into something smaller."

"I'm not sure if you realize this or not but we spend more time at your house than we do our own. Having you move into something smaller will only make your new place crowded." Dad laughed and said that was what his mom had said. "Well, as usual, she's right. Since the ones of us with mates have a home, you'd be better off having Amy do the work, she is the best there is and then seeing if you can get one of the others to move in. If that's really what you want to do."

"It is. Your grandparents have been able to find their own space recently and have decided that the house has too many stairs in it for them. I guess it does. I never really gave it much thought before they mentioned it. After I told your mother, she said she'd been thinking the same thing. And she would love something smaller so that she could have the grandkids over and not have them putting out bread crumbs to find our way to them. I never thought the house was that big but she's got her heart set on something much smaller and with a nice big pool. We so love watching the kids play in yours this summer."

"I have, too. It's been a great deal of fun for all of us." He didn't mention that he and Londyn had been enjoying the pool in the dark of the night for making love, but he had a feeling that his dad, a man who usually thought outside the box about sex and talking to them about it, that he figured it out on his own. "We're having a pool house put in soon. Just to be able to store things in during the colder months. Also, Londyn and I want to get a pontoon boat to travel up and down the river with the kids. You know how much we all love the water."

"I do. Oh some of the trips that we've had over the years. It makes me sometimes sad that you've all grown up and moved on." He told his dad that they'd never move on because they had them to keep them on their toes. "I hope that's true when you all have families of your own."

"Dad, we all have families of our own in you and mom and the grandparents. That will never change." Dad told him he was making himself sobby. "I know what you mean, I'm feeling that way as well right now. Why don't you and Mom meet Londyn and me in town to have some dinner? I know you guys haven't been out in a while, and it will be a blast for the four of us to get together."

"I'd like that. Very much." He told him that he would as well. "Let me talk to your mother and see if she has any plans. I doubt that she'd let that get in the way of spending time with her boys. But you never know."

"She'll have fun too." They made plans for Dad to get back with him as he finished up his part of the shopping. Londyn was nearby in the building next door, looking for things for her new office. She'd decided that working for the family was the only way that she was going to enjoy herself and was pleased that Dad had given her all his law books. Some of them were fairly old, but they were perfect for her. She'd never had her own books, not that many anyway and was excited to build up her own library. He told her what was going on when they met for lunch.

"This will be awesome. I have found myself a desk at the second hand shop. It looks like something that your dad might well have had in his own offices. But I got such a good deal on it that even if it was ugly, I could put up with it. But it's not. I love it, and it's going to be perfect for my new offices. I did get me a new chair however." He told her that he'd gotten another stool for the shop, too, that had a back on it this time. "I don't know how you guys stood, not having a back on your chairs there. I would have been unable to move much after getting up from it." He told her that he rarely sat down, nor did the grandparents and that was probably the reason for it.

"Grandda called me too. He told me that he's been really good at not giving away too much stuff today. I swear that if they worked more than a couple of days a month there each, I'd be in the poor house. They do love to help other people. But they keep good records of things, too. Making sure not to give too much away to one family.

Then they'll expect it, and that won't be good for anyone." She asked him if they did that a lot, gave away things. "Not really. I did have herbs in the spring and when they were finished up with them, they paid some kid around to plant them around the building. It's been nice, but looking over the receipts, I can see where they were giving one away for every one they sold."

"My goodness." They both laughed, and he leaned back in his chair to stare at his mate. "You're looking like a bird who is surveying his prey. Do I have to remind you that we're in public?"

"No. I wasn't...well, I was thinking about sex, but not at that moment. I was thinking about something my dad said about having our own families. I did remind him that he was still a part of the family, with all of us finding our mates. Did you hear that Booth found his mate in a friend of Cullen's?"

"I did hear that. I'm so happy for the two of them. I only hope that he'll be able to heal her when the time is right. I can't imagine what she must be going through right now." Waylon told his own mate that he wasn't sure that she knew that she was paralyzed. "That's more than likely for the best. I mean, she is going through a great deal right now. I'd want to know right away, but I'd also not want to know. Does that make sense?"

"It does. You'd want to know but would be afraid of knowing. Cullen has a connection with her, and I'm not sure what she might know or not now that I think about it. I can see him talking to her and letting her know what the doctors are saying. I would as her friend." She asked him how long they'd known one another. "Years, I guess. I think they were going on a date and figured out that it wasn't for them. I can see that as well. They're good friends that are just that. Very good friends."

"I've never had a friend like that. I wish I did. Someone that I could have spoken to about anything." He pointed out that he was her friend. "Yes, you are, but it's not the same. They'll be able to talk about other people and how much they get on their nerves. You can't be that honest and open when talking about family with family." He still didn't understand but changed the subject.

"I've only a few more things that I need to get. Mostly, it's a new cash register. No one is going to like the change, but they'll get used to it.

Or I'll end up with a lot of cash on the counter with slips of paper on what was sold. It's supposed to help with inventory and will have a special key for when my granddas give things away I can still take it out of inventory. The other day, I read a note from my grandda Sherman that just said paint stuff. That's not very helpful, if you can imagine." They both laughed. "He tried very hard, but there are times when I want to beg him not to come to work. I think they'd be sad if they couldn't be there on their days. They honestly think that they're helping me and I would hate to not have them around to talk to."

"I bet they're a hoot to work with, too. Or do they work alone?" He told her how he had about a dozen high school kids who worked with them so they'd not have to do any heavy lifting. Also, they were able to keep track of the things that went out the door when they were working. "That's good. I can't imagine trying to tell them no, that they can't give things away anymore. I think it would break their hearts."

"It would, I think. Especially when they figure out it's for a good cause. A couple of years ago, while at work, Grandda Sheppard contacted a friend of his to plow up Mr. Martin's ground so he could put in a garden. Then he gave them all the plants and seeds he'd need. Didn't a day go by that Mr. Martin wasn't bringing in something that he'd picked for us. They still talk about how he died that fall after getting everything brought in and saved up. But then it's always a good cause when they're busy giving things away." Again, they both laughed, and he had to stand up they'd been laughing so hard. "We should get finished up if we want to be on time with having dinner with my mom and dad. Dad contacted me a little while ago and told me that Mom was very excited. She wants to go to the garden show nearby and find herself some roses to plant in the garden. My mom has been in garden shows for years and usually comes home with one or two ribbons."

After lunch, they went their separate ways. She was finished up with shopping for her office but she wanted to look for things to put in the spare rooms that had been done up for guests. He didn't know who they'd have staying with them as their family was right there with them, but she was having fun, and he loved watching her enjoy herself all the time.

By the time they were both about shopped out, it was time to meet his parents at the restaurant. He knew that they'd arrived earlier than planned but was able to meet them when it came time for his mom to find her flowers. They'd be delivered next spring and planted in the gardens that she'd had laid out for them. His mom loved a beautiful garden, and he was glad that she was able to get some great deals on them, too. He'd made arrangements to have an herb garden for their cook, and both he and Londyn were thrilled about that.

Dinner was great and he was delighted that his parents enjoyed the place they'd picked out. Having a salad bar in the place, something that he'd not seen in some time, he was happy with just having a go at it. However, he did eat some chicken and loved the lemony sauce that had been seared onto it. None of them drank alcohol, but it was great tea, and they were very happy with that. For dessert he had a nice bowl of ice cream while Londyn had a lovely piece of lemon meringue pie. He was able to have a taste of it and envied that she'd gotten the last piece. After dinner, they were walking around the outside mall and enjoying the evening's slightly cooling weather.

"Won't be long, and it'll be the holidays again. I can't believe that." Londyn told his mom that she had already seen a lot of Christmas décor out in the shops, and it was sad to her. "By the time the holidays are here, I'm about as burnt out on them as I am when summer is over and we're getting ready for fall. I want them to be ready for one season and holiday at a time, but I doubt that they're going to listen to me, some grouchy old ape that has seen better times."

"I don't know that you're grouchy nor old, but I understand what it is you're talking about. Don't get me started on black Friday. It used to be such a wonderful way to get out and get into the spirit of things, but now they start it well before Halloween, and all the charm of getting up at four in the morning is all gone. Not to mention getting better deals on the internet when they call it cyber weeks. What happened to cyber Monday?"

"You two are sounding a little disgruntled. How about if we agree to disagree with the way things have gone and make the best of the seasons. I know for a fact that I'm not going to be bored nor overwhelmed by the seasons if I can help it."

Dad snorted and said that once the children came along if they were to have any, then they'd see how things really were for the holidays.

They all did end up at the Christmas shop that was along the main street. It was beautiful the way that they had it all decorated, and with all the trees set up, he couldn't help but to be ready to rush home and put up his own tree. However, the moment that he stepped outside in the warm evening, he had a dose of reality that made him second guess his decisions about tree decorating and lights around the house.

They were getting home around ten when he remembered that he had to unload his car. With them working together, the two of them were in bed at about eleven o'clock and asleep not too long after. It had been a long day and evening, and he, for one, was thrilled to be able to not just get into their bed but to put their feet up as well.

Their hot tub was being delivered and set up tomorrow. One more day and he figured that he could get himself relaxed enough that he'd not toss and turn so much. What with the new things coming in and the things going on with the newest addition to the family, he was about as beat as he'd ever been before. He was thrilled to no end that he had a place to unwind and relax like he did in his new home that wasn't overwhelmed with family all the time. He loved them but they were a bit much when you were stressing out.

He had to get up twice in the middle of the night. Having all that good tea was something that he was paying for. Getting back into his bed the second time, he was happy to snuggle up to Londyn. Having her as his mate and friend was making him see things that he'd not before. Like how much his parents really and truly loved one another. And they did.

As they walked in front of them tonight, looking at the displays in the windows about sales coming up, they held each other's hands. It wasn't new to him to see them catching a kiss or two. He'd been amazed at his parents all his life and how much they loved to show how much they loved one another like they did. Even at football games, they were affectionate and loving. It used to embarrass him, but now all he could think about was that he'd love to have a love like they did. Where other people's opinions mattered to them and they loved each other like they did with everything they did. They loved each other like they did and damn the consequences of anyone else opinion about them.

It made him want to be like them. And he decided that from now on he was going to show his love and support for all his family, not just his mate. Life was too unexpected and there was no point in his life to think that he should have done things differently when he had all the time in the world to love and to be loved. And Waylon did love his family with all that he was.

~*~

Londyn was thrilled with the way that her office was looking. She had an office in the downtown area, a place where she could have an office front in the event she was needed for the family, but having this lovely office at home was making her happy that she wasn't going to be stuck in an office all day but to be able to deal with things as they came up and still be at home in the event Waylon or one of their children needed her when they came along.

Putting the little finishing touches around the room, photographs that she took with her phone of Waylon and his family in pretty frames.

Pieces of things that she picked up while out with him too. A ticket stub here, some pretty stones from the beach that they'd gone to for an afternoon of boating. Little things that would mean very little to anyone else, but to her, they meant the world.

"Do you have time to—good heavens, Londyn, this is beautiful. I'm jealous that I didn't have you do my office once I decided to have one at home." She told Sherman, Waylon's dad, that she was pleased with how it turned out as well. "My goodness, I love all the little touches. And the flowers are just the perfect touch to make the room seem less office like and more like a meeting place for anyone that comes in."

"Thank you. I figured that if I was going to have an office at home, I make it something that I'd not avoid." He said he thought he'd done that as well. "What is it that you wanted me to look over."

"Oh, yes. It's the testimony of the man who sued Waylon about the house he wanted to have built. I know that there isn't going to be a trial anytime soon, if ever, but he says some things in it that make me wonder if this isn't the way that he does things. Makes a few comments to people and then sues them when things don't go his way." She earmarked the things that he said that he wanted her to look over in favor of talking to Sherman. He was a brilliant man, she had discovered, and he loved history and the law.

"We took your advice and had our license filed about us being married. It was much easier than I thought it would be, and now it's all done. Amy said that she's having a large wedding in a few months for her and Jayden to tie the knot and that her brother is insisting that it be in the White House. I couldn't handle all that going on." He told her that he wasn't sure that he could either. "I guess when your sister of the president, there isn't much you can do to make your life quiet."

He told her how she had tried to stay out of the limelight when she'd been living at her own home, but it didn't work out all that well for them. Now that it was out and about, it also served to hide away the relationship that Jamie had with his mother. Or the one that she thought that they'd have together.

"Yes, that was a mess from the start. The poor woman had her own terror of living at her childhood home, and that is what made her like she was." She told him that she'd heard about it from Hazel. At least some of it. "I'm sure that she glossed over a great deal of it. Keeping it out of the paper had been the hardest on Jamie. Poor man. He and Carol or finally getting their life on track with their two little ones."

They talked about different things for the next half hour. When he left her, she got to work on the paperwork that he'd brought her and made notes on the things that he'd pointed out to her. Once she had the notes, she turned them over to the man who was running the show when it came to suing Waylon about his home. She thought that it was a done deal that he was going to jail but she hadn't kept up on things while she'd been hanging around her mate.

After she had finished up for the day, going to the kitchen to find out what plans had been made for dinner, she was told that they were going to cook out salmon and was happy about that. That was one of the things that she loved more than salads was grilled salmon and rice.

Going out to the pool, she dead headed some of the flowers that had lost their blooms and sat around the lovely area in favor of being in the house. Since meeting and falling in love with Waylon, she found that she loved the outdoors more than before, and her meals had changed as well. She enjoyed a nice green salad over having much in the way of meat and desserts. Even though she had one, it wasn't much of a hardship to give up, either.

Heading home, the four of them hugged tightly before getting into their cars. It was an evening that she'd not soon forget, and was glad that they had made the time to join them. She was going to make sure that she and Waylon did this more often, just meeting up with his parents for a night out. It made the days seem so much better when you had something so wonderful to look forward to and to remember.

By the time they were home, it was dark enough that they had to use the flashlights on their phones to see the steps. Going inside and locking up, they didn't even bother to look at the mail but simply went up to bed and fell exhausted into the bed. It was the first time since they'd been sleeping together that they didn't make love before going to sleep. Exhaustion had a way of making them feel like they needed sleep over sex, she supposed.

The next morning, she was waiting for the things to be delivered when her cell phone rang. It occurred to her that she'd not made a connection with the rest of the family when she spoke to Cullen. He wanted to know if he could meet her for lunch today. All for spending time with him, they arranged to meet at her office and he told her that he'd be there by noon. It was just nine now, and she was excited to be able to help this member of the family out.

He arrived just as her boxes did, and once he got them into the room where they belonged, he sat at her new desk and smiled at her. She wasn't sure of his smiles yet but was willing to think that it was a good one when he started speaking.

"The government wants me to reenlist. I'm not going to do it but they sent me a contract over that says some gibberish about how I can't work for any other government agency so long as I live. I'm not sure why they'd think after all the time that I've spent with them that I'd go rogue on them, but that's what I'm getting from the first read-over of the contract. If you could give it a good look, I'd appreciate it." She asked him if he had it on him. Once the file was in her hands, she realized right off the bat that the wording of the first line was off. "What do you mean by off?"

"They're saying that not only can you be tried with treason but that they can have you brought for a firing squad if you decided to do anything that the contract here forbids you to do. I'd not sign it simply for that reason. Firing squad? Do they even do that anymore?" He didn't so much as blink at her. "Thank you for not answering that. But no, I'd not sign this."

She read over the rest of the contract, and she picked up her phone and called Jamie. She'd been told to do that when she had questions, and she was reasonably sure that he had no idea that they were going to do things like this contract said to Cullen if he were to simply step into another office of the government. He answered her with a laugh, and she had to smile.

After reading to him what was in the first couple of paragraphs, he asked her to fax it to him. She told him that according to the contract, he couldn't fax it anywhere or he'd be killed.

"I don't like this. Send it over, and I'll take care that nothing happens to him. Nor you. Christ, this sounds like something that another country would do to my boy." She sent it to him, then sat back and waited for him to get it. "I'm going to read this over and—ah yes, it is signed. Good. This won't take me but a few hours to get to the bottom of. Let me call you both back when I have this straightened out. Arrogant people drive me insane."

While they waited on the callback, Cullen helped her put her things in the right places. He was extremely helpful in moving her desk to the window, being that he was as strong as...well, an ape. Plus he was able to get the boxes broken down quickly and efficiently without much in the way of mess. She loved that he was a clean as he went person. She might well have been overwhelmed if not for him being there helping. By the time they got the call back from Jamie, they had the office situated and ready for her first job. Second, she supposed, counting Cullen.

"I've spoken to the man, General Briggs, and he's decided to retire as of today." Jamie laughed, but it wasn't full of humor like one would expect. "The man thought that he was doing the country a favor by making sure that our best man wasn't going to the other side. As it is now, he's lucky that he still has his pension as well as the ability to retire, like I'm allowing him to do. Stupid man."

"Cullen wants to get out of the service. I believe, too, that he's done plenty for his country and deserves his pension as well as his retirement. If you have a problem with that, then I'll have no trouble taking you on either." Cullen laughed, and she smiled at him. "Are you going to have a problem with that?"

"Not at all. I was going to suggest that you write up a contract that favors him, but I have a feeling that you'll have him living in the White House with me so that he can keep an eye on me for the time I have left."

"Damned straight." They all three laughed and she was glad that it turned out so well that she was going to make this as her first win. Not that she had a great deal to do with it, but it was finished up in Cullen's favor, and that was a win so far as she was concerned.

Chapter 8

Booth watched Lydia's face after the doctor told her that she was paralyzed. He could see disbelief on her face as well as bits of anger. The thing that the doctor didn't know or seem to understand was that she was healing. Just this morning, he'd noticed that she could wiggle her toes. A large feat if you asked him about it.

"Do you have any questions, Lydia?" She just stared at the doctor. "I know this is a great deal to take in, but we're all here for you should you think of something later that you have questions about. We're here for you."

The doctor was gone for a good twenty minutes before she turned and looked at him. There was pain there, not from her body but from her heart. She asked him what was going to happen to her now.

"I'm not sure what that means." She told him that she wasn't going to be able to walk again, not to mention to have sex. "Yes, well, I'm not sure that you have to worry about any of that. I told you yesterday that you wiggled your toes. I think that once I'm able to claim you, as my gorilla really wants to do, then you're going to see vast improvements all over your body."

"How do you know." He touched his finger to her toe and asked her if she could feel it. "Yes, but that's just my toe, not my legs. I wouldn't count that as a big win when I'm not going to be able to do anything other than to just sit around in a wheelchair for the rest of my life. And from what you told me yesterday, that's going to be forever."

The day before yesterday and last night again, they'd talked about her being his mate. She sometimes had to have him repeat it several times, but he thought for sure that she understood that now. Sometimes, she'd ask him a question that he'd answered before, but that was all right as well. It was a great deal to take in, and a lot of stress going along with it. Today was just for him answering questions after the doctor left. He didn't much care for the man. He seemed like he had more important things to do other than to answer questions for her but with Falkner around most of the time, they were understanding more and more about what was going on than when he'd been explaining it to them.

Just as he was thinking of his younger brother, he walked into the door with not just food for the three of them, but he told her that he had good news for them as well. There wasn't any time for them to eat as Lydia was peppering him with questions about what he'd been able to find out.

"There is swelling along your spine that is causing the paralysis. I'm not entirely sure where he got that you had a broken back, but it looks like the swelling is going down." He looked at her with a wink. "There was a break in your spine, but since Booth has been hanging around with you more and more, it looks as if you're healing on your own. With his magic, I guess."

"I've been meaning to ask you something. Do you heal your patients when you're around them?" Good question, he thought and waited on his answer with Lydia. "I mean, he's just been hanging around, as you said, which I have to say, he must have more important things to do other than that, but he won't leave, and I guess I'm fine with that too. He's like some old mold. He's beginning to grow on me."

"I'm betting that he loves hearing that too. But no, I don't heal them because they're not my mate. Nor have I claimed them as my family." He laughed. "I actually thought of that as well when I first started out. But no, I don't heal them unless it's by prescription or other means. But that is a great question. How are you dealing with all of this?"

"I have no idea. One minute, I'm all right. The next, I'm upset that that man hurt me and thinks that he should be treated special because of what he is. Bastard. I wonder how he treats his family." Booth answered that question for her. "Just as I thought. He's a bastard to everyone he's around. His poor family must be happy that he's in jail right now. I know that I am."

By the time Falkner left, she was able to bend her ankle. Being told to take it easy so that she'd not be sore, she told him that she wanted so badly to get out of bed and dance. Not that she could, but that was what she wanted to do more than anything. Just get out and move.

After Falkner left them, they didn't speak for a while. Booth did hold her hand. There was something so comforting about it that he watched as she started to drift off. By the time she was sleeping soundly, he was getting tired himself. It had been a long few days, and he wanted to take her home with him and heal her completely. But this way was better. She'd be healing a little at a time and that wouldn't make anyone suspicious about her being better so quickly.

Getting up to walk around, his body becoming stiff just sitting there, he went to the window and looked out onto the gardens below. There were staff out there having their lunch, and he watched as they fed the birds some of their crumbs. Laughing when one of the bolder birds landed on the table they were sitting on, he managed to get away with nearly half a slice of bread and take it to the trees where he was sure his family was. Animals were a great distraction when it came to having to think about the bad news that this entire thing could have been.

Booth thought about the translations he was doing for the government. They'd been able to find more papers in the small room that had been discovered. For their cooperation in letting the government have the paperwork that they'd found, they were paying for the renovation of the house for the couple. They were more than a little pleased with the arrangements and Booth was happy about it as well. It seemed like they were all coming out ahead on this.

"Did you know that you talk to yourself?" He turned and smiled at Lydia. "I thought that you were talking to me, but then I realized that you weren't. What are you talking about that seems so important to you?"

He told her about the papers that had been found and anything else about the work that he was going to cheer her up. He also told her that he'd been able to find several more recipes in the same hand and that he was going to find someone to cook them for him. The one that he really wanted was the roast quail with pine nuts.

"I don't think that I've ever had quail of pine nuts, but the little bits of notes that they put in the lines of ingredients that make me think that I'll like it." She asked him about the notes. "It's funny really. It talks about how an aunt doesn't care for the nuts, so they have to leave them out for her and that one of the nephews doesn't care for quail, so they tell him that it's chicken and he's been devouring it."

"My grandma used to do that to me. Tell me it was chicken when it wasn't. We had lamb one year for easter. I don't have to tell you what a disaster that was for us. My questioning mind wanted to know why there were these large lamb chops when I hadn't ever seen a chicken with a chop before. Turns out she finally had to tell me the truth, and I never trusted her about chicken or food for that matter ever again." He told her about broccoli and how he had hated it until he tried it. "Yes, I can see a kid doing that. Broccoli does look odd, and to think that it's a vegetable is really off-putting. For me, anyway."

They talked about their childhood, getting around to her injuries as well. When she seemed to be drifting off again, he didn't say anything to her but watched as her eyes closed slower and slower. When it seemed that she was out, he pulled himself over a chair and began reading some more of the transcripts.

The notes, like he'd observed before seemed to have been jots of notes that someone wrote down to remember something for later. The author, a man by the name of William S. Prater, would also cut out clippings of the paper and put them into his notes as well. There were a great deal of misspelled words as well as his translation of things, like the billboards that he would read, was a bit off but he usually got the drift of things and did a good job. It was enjoyable to him and to Jamie about how much the man seemed to have an opinion about nearly everything, from politics to the growing of apples.

Reading a passage about the weather, it was cold, and the snow was piling up. He went on to explain how he was going to go through his wood before the season was nearly over. Also, he seemed to have a good accounting of the people in town, too. The man was a savant gossiper as well as someone who was free with his opinions about how people raised their children.

Since he did mention several times that he had none of his own, it was also funny to him that he thought that he could do a much better job than anyone else when it came to disciplining them as well. He was a 'spare the rod, spoil the child' sort of man.

There were prices of cattle, pigs, and corn that he would ruminate about as well. He felt that if he were in charge of such things, the country would be better off not paying the farmers for their product because it was for the good of the country. Booth had to laugh when he figured out on his own that it was farmers who kept the world going and that not paying them could and would lead to harder times. He also didn't mind admitting when he was wrong either. Which, by Booth's accounting, wasn't all that often.

When he had about enough of William, he'd turn to looking things up on the internet. Nothing as profoundly as what he was reading but just little tidbits of things that he thought were interesting. Nothing to do with politics or the price of grain. He liked thinking that he was living in a time when he could afford to be a part of both and not have to worry about the consequences of talking about either or both of them.

Like his brothers, he loved to go to auctions and found one on Saturday that he might want to go to. There wasn't any real estate for the auction, but he did look it up when it mentioned the realtor. Finding out the name of the place that was representing the family involved, he called them up and asked about the house. It was for sale, but she, a nice woman said that she thought that they were asking entirely too much for the house and it wouldn't sell without a lot of work done on it too.

"The kitchen dates back to the eighties. There is carpet throughout the place that should have been replaced decades ago. Also, the roof needs to be replaced as well as the furnace and air. I'd not buy it for the asking price. I know that it's a sale for me but they're asking prices of the place when it was a booming town. We're not that anymore around here." He asked her the price. "Nearly half a million. Also, I forgot to mention that there is nothing in the way of land either. A quarter of an acre is all. It's not going to sell unless they drop the price to about a tenth of that. And maybe not even then."

"What can you tell me about the contents?" She told him that the last that she'd heard, they had a minimum price on everything, and even that was too high. "I see. So there is going to be a lot of standing around and no one getting any good deals. I'll pass."

"I don't blame you, Booth. But wait a moment. If you're looking for a house, I have one that's not even on the market yet. The family just decided last weekend that they wanted to sell. Let me get the paperwork for you." When she came back on the line not only did she have an address but told him that she'd meet him out there if he wanted to go. "I'm supposed to meet another couple out there in an hour, but they've been changing the time for the last several days. If you want to meet me there in about half an hour, I can go over the house with you even if they don't show up."

"Great. I have to get someone to watch over my mate here, so I'll meet you there." He reached out to his dad and told him what he was doing. When he said that he and his mom were in town, they were there before he got off the phone with Bonnie Andrews. "I have someone coming in. As soon as they arrive, I'll drive out."

Lydia woke up just as he was leaving. After telling her what was going on, she wished that she could go with him. While she knew that she couldn't he did promise her that he'd take lots of pictures of the place so that he could show it to her. Once he was at the house, he thought for sure that he had the wrong place. The front lawn of the place looked like it was doubling as a trash heap, and there were garbage bags all over the front of the street as well. He was ready to leave when Bonnie showed up.

"I swear it didn't look like this when I was given the paperwork on it." She handed him what she had. "Look? There isn't even a front porch on the place much less this mess. There has to be a mistake here, and if you give me a few minutes, I'll get to the bottom of this. I have a feeling that no one has been out here since these pictures were taken a few months ago."

He stayed near his car as she talked to her home office. While waiting, he pulled out his phone and began looking at the other auctions that were going on. He wasn't going to go to the one that had a price listed for items, but now that he'd thought about it, he wanted to hit one up, if for no other reason than to get out and around people who would be excited to be there.

People, as far as he could understand, were of two minds when it came to auctions. They were there to either flip the stuff they bought or were looking for a good deal on things for their own home or someone else's and were tight with their cash. He was in the latter of the two. He wanted a good deal for a good item.

He found three that he had earmarked for this coming weekend and Bonnie had found out that the address had been printed wrong on all the paperwork. Even the contracts that had been from the other couple had been wrong. She pointed to the correct house, just one street over, and they headed that way.

As soon as he pulled into the drive, he was in love. Sending a picture of the front of the house to Lydia via his father's phone, she called him right away. He was laughing even as he got out of his car and telling her about the mess up.

"Good. I mean, I love it when a person admits that they made a mistake. I'll be happy to work with someone like her." He told her that he would as well and put the chat on video so that she could see the house as he did. It was a good deal more exciting than he thought it would have been buying himself a house.

~*~

Lydia was glad that he was making her a part of the buying of the house. Not that she was ready to move in with him yet, but it was fun to think that they were this far along in their relationship.

Not that they had one as yet but they were slowly working on it.

"I don't much care for the front doors. They'll have to go." She asked him what was wrong with them. "They're all right in that they're double doors, but they're just wood, and if I were going to be greeting people when they come to the house, I want to see them first."

"Now that you mention it, that is a good idea. And I can almost see a glass-fronted door decorated at Christmas, too. With all kinds of lights and such." He said he'd never decorated at Christmas before as he only lived in an apartment. "We'll have to go all out if we get the house. Or any house, for that matter. I've not had a good Christmas in about a decade. Not to mention, your brother Cullen will be home this year so that'll be fun to go all out with him around."

"I love that idea." The kitchen in the place was going to need some work. It looked as if someone had started on it and then gave up about halfway through the project. He told her that he cooked and asked her if she did. "Not so much as I'd depend on me cooking for us nightly. I can only cook things that I have a good recipe for, but nothing while trying to wing it. Your mom was telling me that she has a nice herb garden that she uses year-round, and Waylon is going to have one put in for him as well. I don't know that I'd venture that far."

They talked about the house and the yard. There was a fenced in backyard but no pool. Neither of them knew if they wanted one or not but thought that they could get to that later. They both liked that it had six big bedrooms and bathrooms as well as a back porch that was completely screened in with a dry bar and large grill. That was something that he would look forward to more than anything.

"The house has a new furnace." Bonnie told them both of all the new things that the house had, as well as a couple of things that it would need immediately. The grounds would need to be brought back up to something manageable as well as the garage. There was an apartment over the garage that would serve as a nice office, but since he didn't really need one and he didn't know what it was that Lydia did for a living, they let it go for now. He'd find out that information later when they were talking more together.

They decided to make an offer on the house

right away before the other paperwork was given to the other couple, and she said that she'd get back to him. He didn't know if the offer would be accepted. It was far below what was being asked but with the work that needed to be done, it was good for him. He asked her about auctions.

"I've never been to one before. Garage sales? Yes, plenty of them. My sister used to clothe her children with those all the time. I don't know what she does now as she's moved to Europe with her husband and kids. I've not seen her in years. I think that we get along better that way." He told her he did wonder if she had family. "I do. A sister, whom I've mentioned, as well as an older brother. He's nearly old enough to be my dad. Shawn and Lynn. Both are married, though, like I said, I don't see them much. My parents are in Europe as well and I've not spoken to them in longer than my sister and brother. We don't really see eye to eye about a lot of things."

"I'm sorry to hear about that. I don't know what I'd do if I didn't have my family around all the time. Do you expect them to know about your accident? Or that we've met?" She told him that she doubted that they'd care one way or another.

They really didn't get along. "That's so sad. Like I said, I love mine."

They talked about the house and other things on his way back to the hospital. When he arrived, Dad had gone out and gotten them food. Lydia could now bend her knee, and the doctor knew about it. He'd tested her reflexes and found out that she was finally on the mend. They were all happy about that, and she was happy the most. She'd be walking before too much longer and that was something that they could all get behind.

Even though she'd seen the house with the chat, he showed her the pictures that he had taken. Mostly, it was the kitchen, and she agreed with him that it needed to be the most worked on. About the time his parents had left, saying that they'd go with him to the auction on Saturday, they'd heard back from the family that owned the house, and they made a counteroffer.

"I'd say that you should turn him down. Even though what he's asking isn't too much off of what you offered, I'd still wait on your price. It's a good offer, and with the work that you need to pay for, I think he's going to be lucky to get as much as you're offering. However, if he looks as if he's going to walk away, I'll counter with something more reasonable for you." He told her that he liked that idea after talking it over with Lydia. "Also, he's not going to pay for insurance on the house. The kind that if there is something major that needs to be done that wasn't disclosed, it'll pay for it. I'd demand that if I were you. It's a lovely home, and I heard your wife decorating for Christmas, but it's not going to be worth it if you have to put in an entire septic system three days after you close on the house."

He loved Bonnie. And he was going to suggest to everyone that he knew to use her as she was honest and upfront with him about the things going on in the house. She also told him about the other couple canceling on her again, even after giving them the new address of the house.

"I think they just like the idea of buying a house instead of actually buying one. I run into people like that all the time. They like to play at it and not really have the funds nor the wherewithal to get a house no matter what kind of price they get for it." She laughed. "My in-laws are like that. Wanting a new home simply because they're sick of the one they've lived in for the last thirty or so years but don't have the money to move or to be moved. I believe that happens to a lot of older people, too. They realize that they have a house that is much too large for the two of them, and the kids don't want it."

It was late, too late, he thought, for them to hear from the couple that owned the house, so he made his way home after telling Lydia good night. She was doing so much better and he was glad to see that the doctors were making her take it easy with her moving her body. He would claim her soon, just to make sure that all her other wounds were healed. Dad he was glad was able to tell them about the senator and his woes about what was going on with him and the accident.

"He's been arrested and without bond. The amount of coke and things that he had in his truck made them think that he wasn't going to be an easy person to hold in town. So they put him in jail, took his passport from him and his wife, and seized his bank accounts. The man is in for a great deal of money because of the deaths that he caused — two more people have died as a result of the accident, and that's not setting well with anyone." Lydia asked about her situation. "He caused the accident.

It doesn't matter if you healed or not. He was the cause of a great deal of anguish and suffering on your part. Not to mention all the damage that he did to that intersection. There were a great many people hurt solely because of him running a red light."

After Dad and his mom left, Lydia looked pensive. Like she was afraid of the man getting away with basically murder. She asked him what he'd do if it came to her pressing charges or not.

"You did the movement that he ran you into the oncoming traffic, and he caused the accident. You can sue him, too, as well, for what my dad was saying about it but I'd think that there is no way he's going to be getting off the hook anytime soon. If ever. The man is a horrific person, and the sooner he has to pay, the better off the roads, and people driving on them will be safer. Dad seems to think that he'd done something like this before. Maybe not killed anyway, but he'd bet that he'd been responsible for a lot of people injured. He was having his name put out there in other states, too. That might not bring anything, but it might, too. You never know about people." Lydia said that she hated that he had a family that was going to be dragged through all of this. "I bet, if I were them that they're glad that it's out in the open. Like I said, he's more than likely done this before."

On his way home, he thought about the house and the accident. He hated that someone had to be killed in order for him to find his mate and a house where he could live with her in, but things were working out better for them. He only hoped that once this was all cleared up and everything put to rest, the two of them could start to live their lives better all the way around. He was just happy to have found her when he did. Booth had been having a terrible few days before meeting her, and he didn't like those feelings.

Suffering from depression, like most people did, he thought, he didn't much care to be alone with his own thoughts. They were getting him into deeper darkness and he wanted to be out of it as soon as he could. Even if she could only be there to hold his hand for a little while, he thought that it would do him a world of good. Sometimes, that was all it would take for him. To talk to someone or just hang around with them without talking. It brought him out faster than any other thing when it was one of his family that would help him out.

The day that he'd met her had been one of those days. A day when he couldn't seem to get out of his funk in any way. It was like that at times when he just couldn't shake the bad thoughts, but now—he hoped he'd be able to find her and simply hold her hand, and that would help him a great deal. That's what he wanted someone to hold his hand when he needed it most.

There was a message on his house phone when he got home. The couple, like they'd been told, had turned down their offer. Nor were they going to offer insurance on the place. He and Lydia had talked about it, and while he could afford it to have the house repaired if something major came along, they were going to demand at least that much.

Not bothering to call her back, knowing that she had things under control, he went up to his bedroom and took a long shower. After getting in bed, he turned his phone to silent so that he'd not be awakened anytime before nine. He'd been not sleeping well, thanks to the paperwork he'd been doing, and he wanted to be able to be rested when he went to the hospital again tomorrow. Then, the next day, they were going to go to the auction, and he was looking forward to that as much as he was about Lydia coming home. They had a lot to catch up on and a good deal more to talk about, and he couldn't have been happier than he was right at this moment.

AWARD WINNING, BESTSELLING AUTHOR

Kathi Barton, a winner of the Pinnacle Book Achievement Award and a best-selling author on Amazon and All Romance books, lives in Nashport, Ohio, with her husband, Paul. When not creating new worlds and romance, Kathi and her husband enjoy camping and going to auctions. She can also be seen at county fairs with her husband, an artist and potter.

Her muse, a cross between Jimmy Stewart and Hugh Jackman, brings her stories to life for her readers in a way that has them coming back time and again for more. Her favorite genre is paranormal romance, with a great deal of spice. You can visit Kathi online and drop her an email if you'd like. She loves hearing from her fans. aaronskiss@gmail.com.

Follow Kathi on her blog: http://kathisbartonauthor.blogspot.com/